A CRIME - MYSTERY - THRILLER

By

Satyam Srivastava

Rajeev Garg

ISBN 978-81-948043-7-6

First published in India 2021 by Inkstate Books
An imprint of Leadstart Publishing Pvt Ltd

119-123, 1st Floor, Building J2,B - Wing,
Wadala Truck Terminal, Wadala East,
Mumbai 400022, Maharashtra, INDIA
Phone: +91 969933000
Email: info@leadstartcorp.com
www.leadstartcorp.com

Disclaimer: The Views expressed in this book are those of the Author and do not pertain to be held by the Publisher.

Editor: Shayoni Mitra
Cover: Ashwini Jadhav
Layouts: Ashwini Jadhav

My first creation is dedicated to my better half, who is a staunch devotee of Lord Shiva, and my adorable kids. I thank my parents and sisters for their unshrinking love and support. Special gratitude to my Nana, maternal uncles and other family members who enabled me to become the person I am. I shall forever be grateful to my alma maters, IIT Bombay and NADT, for giving wings to my dreams. I shall never forget the trust and confidence bestowed upon me by my friends, teachers and colleagues. They have been the reason I was even able to start this journey.

Satyam

I dedicate this book to my parents and my brother. They are the reason behind what I am today. To all my teachers who instilled in me the love of learning. To my wife, who had to bear my absence when I was busy authoring this book. And to Aakarsh and Aaira, my little twins, whom I want this story to be told, when they grow up.

Rajeev

TABLE OF CONTENTS

PART I

ANTĀRAMBHA
(BEGINNING OF THE END)

यदा यदा हि धर्मस्य ग्लानिर्भव – ति भारत ।
अभ्युत्थान– मधर्मस्य तदात्मानं सृजाम्यहम ।।
परित्राणाय– साधूनां विनाशाय च दुष्कृताम ।
धर्मसंस्था– पनार्थाय सम्भवामि युगे युगे ।।

जब जब भी धर्म का विनाश हुआ, अधर्म का उत्थान हुआ,
तब तब मैंने खुद का सृजन किया, साधुओं के उद्धार और
बुरे कर्म करने वालो के संहार के लिए,
धर्म की स्थापना के प्रयोजन से, मै हर युग में, युग युग में जनम लेता रहूँगा ।

Whenever, O descendant of Bharata, there is decline of
Dharma, and rise of Adharma, then I body Myself forth. For
the protection of the good, for the destruction of the wicked,
and for the establishment of Dharma I come into being in
every age.

[Bhagavad Gita, Chapter 4, Verse 7-8]

Chapter 1
DAMAḤ
(RESTRAINT)

North Block
June 10, 1:08 PM

It is the afternoon of another warm, humid day in Delhi.

A white Honda Civic stops at Gate 3 of the North Block. An armed security guard rushes to open the door. A tall uniformed man of average build steps out. He looks at the power center of the nation and takes a deep breath. Even though he has visited this building numerous times before, today is different. The Home Minister has summoned him. Such meetings are not among the routine ones.

The security guard gives a salute, "Jai Hind, sir. Mantriji (minister) is waiting for you."

He acknowledges the salute and puts his cap on. Mantriji is informed, as he alights.

Office, Home Minister
June 10, 1:20 PM

"I expected more from you Ajay." The tone of the Home Minister, Manohar Ghosh, is stern. Special Commissioner of Police (Crime Branch) or Spl. CP (Crime) Ajay Raj Singh corrects his posture pushing his medal embellished chest to the full view of Mantriji, as if to remind him of his past achievements.

But Manohar does not seem to care.

"Sir, we have deputed our best resources to this case. They will not disappoint you."

"It has been three days since her disappearance. Your team has been ineffective. This is the third case in this month alone, where your investigation has gone nowhere." The calmness now breaks into a growl.

"Sir, we have zeroed down on some suspects. But such cases take time."

"Find your motivation back Ajay, otherwise North-East will get a new Commissioner of Police soon." Spl. CP Ajay Raj Singh could feel the growl breaking into a threat. Transfer is the ultimate weapon, a *brahmāstra*, in the hands of any minister. No bureaucrat can afford to take this threat lightly. But Ajay seems unperturbed. *Won't happen…* he thinks to himself. *The two of us go way back...*

"We are trying our best, sir."

"Apparently, not enough. The media is going bonkers. I cannot take any more pressure. They have started demanding my resignation. I need to show some action. Immediate transfer of the team will at least convey that I am acting!"

"Sir, please give us more time."

"A luxury I don't have, Ajay. I want results. Next time I hear from you, I want some news. And it better be good."

After a brief pause, he adds, "And it better be soon." The Minister's tone is harsh, and it conveys the message loud and clear.

Ajay leaves the room knowing that failure is not an acceptable option now.

Police Headquarters
June 10, 3:30 PM

Ajay's lunchbox has remained untouched and he has already sipped four coffees since coming back.

In a sense, he is happy that the day has finally come. The timing of the proposal had to be perfect, else it would have been shot down without any deliberation. Every bureaucrat waits for such moments. They can be career defining. Ajay knows that this is the right time.

Ajay unlocks the drawer in his table and takes out a folder. He opens it and reads the one-page brief one more time, carefully weighing every word in it. Writing a crisp one-page brief for political bosses is an essential skill for bureaucrats. Precise information must be conveyed with minimum bullet points and Ajay has mastered it with time. He himself has typed it. *No one else can know!* Satisfied, he closes the folder and picks up a black marker from his desk.

Ajay cogitates for more than a minute and then writes

the title. *It is perfect.* The folder then goes back into the drawer.

He picks up his smartphone and calls Mantriji, instead of the landline, signaling the urgency of the call. After the exchange of greetings, Ajay speaks, "Sir, I may have a solution. You may not like it."

"Let me be the judge of that. Speak."

"Sir, we need to speak in person."

Mantriji doesn't like such cryptic replies, but he agrees reluctantly, "Alright. My office. 5 PM."

Office, Home Minister
June 10, 5:10 PM

Ajay pushes a folder titled 'PROJECT KAALI' to Mantriji. It bears the insignia 'TOP SECRET – HM's Eyes only'. Manohar starts to read.

His eyes widen as he moves from one line to another. He stops midway and blurts, "Ajay, you can't be serious. What you are asking of me is not legal!"

"Sir, with due respect, the crime rate has crossed all limits. The city has had enough. Time is of essence in such cases. Desperate times call for desperate measures."

Sensing that Mantriji is not convinced, he adds, "We will take due precautions, sir. None of this will ever be known to the public."

Manohar continues to read.

"Will it work?"

"I am sure, sir."

"But won't the suspects tell everyone?"

"No, sir. I have a way."

The restlessness on the face of Mantriji is evident. Ajay continues, "Sir, if we want quick results, we need this Kaali to stop these criminals." Ajay, a seasoned bureaucrat, has named the folder purposely so, giving a reference to revered Goddess Kaali. He knows very well that this is the language a devout Bengali would understand.

"It will be a surgical strike on crime, sir."

"And what will you call this unit?"

"SARP - Special Anti-crime and Research Program."

"SARP – A new acronym; it seems you too have picked up the habit of making fancy sounding acronyms. I hope it won't turn out to be just another acronym."

"Sir, it will be a small elite response team comprising of handpicked officers to investigate serious and high-profile crimes with its own research lab and some special powers."

Some special powers, smirks Mantriji.

"But what you are asking is not legit."

"Sir, enough of restraint. Someone has to start taking the tough decisions."

North Block

June 10, 5:45 PM

Ajay walks out of the North Block and looks at the setting sun. *That was easier than I thought,* he thinks as he lights up a cigarette and calmly finishes it. It is time to make the call. He takes out his cell phone and makes a call to the last dialed number.

"Project Kaali is a go. Only change is the name of the

unit. We will call it CIU - Crime Investigation Unit, as per Mantriji's wishes. It is time to take your Schrodinger's cat out of the box and see if it is alive."

Office, Home Minister
June 10, 9:35 PM

A pile of files are lying on the desk for his approval and signatures. The peon has already cleared two such stacks in the last one hour. It has been a long day for Manohar. Just when he is done with the last of the signatures and is about to leave the office, he receives a call from Ajay.

"Yes, Ajay."

"Please put on the news, sir."

Manohar switches on the TV.

... The high-profile kidnapping case of the son of business tycoon Roshan Khanna has been cracked. The child is safe and is being returned to the family by the police authorities. The culprit, none other than the child's uncle, has been caught and ...

"Good job, Ajay. I knew you would rise to the occasion. I had full faith in your abilities."

"Sir, it was all due to your leadership and the ability to take tough decisions," a typical bureaucratic response but this time Ajay really means it. It is also to subtly remind the minister of the risk he has taken.

They both know that *the line* has been crossed.

Chapter 2
Ārambha
(The Start)

Office, Noida
July 7, 7:45 AM

It is a pleasant July morning. Petrichor has filled the air. Delhi-NCR (National Capital Region) has finally broken the monotony of hot sweltering summers and is experiencing its first monsoon showers of the season.

An auto rickshaw stops at the headquarters of News 360 channel. Dressed in black trousers, a white top and a dark jacket, a nervous looking Kritika gets down. Her neatly braided hair get wet by the blowing drizzle. Such fond have been her memories of rains, that the inner child in her wants to drop the pencil heels and start dancing in the rain. Instead she looks at her watch and rushes into the building.

It is her first day in the new office. As she comes out of the elevator, she sees a large hall with many workstations. In the hall, there are many TV screens showing parallel feeds of various other English news channels. Some chairs are empty, but the hall has a busy feel about it. She sees the glass door to the office of Aditya Bajaj, the Content Manager, her new boss.

The receptionist notices Kritika. She gets up and extends her hand.

"Good morning Kritika. Welcome to News 360."

"Good morning." The handshake is soft.

"I am Rashmi."

"Hi Rashmi."

Rashmi hands over a card. "This is your ID card. Let me show you your station."

Kritika takes the ID card and wears it around her neck and starts to walk behind Rashmi.

She stops between two stations. "This is your station."

Kritika reads her name on the station. She puts her bag down and takes a look. It is exactly how she has imagined. A comfortable looking chair, a table with a laptop and two telephone handsets and a three-drawer cabinet under the table.

"You have a meeting at 8:15 AM in that room." She points to the corner room at the end of the hall.

Kritika sits on her chair. She looks around and reads the names 'Rakesh Dhawan' and 'Shivani Kaur'. The chairs are empty. There is a folder on her table. She opens the folder. It is a welcome kit. It has a pack of visiting cards, a pen with News 360 inscribed on it, a booklet with both cell-phone and intercom numbers of her colleagues, a notepad and an appointments diary. She takes out a visiting card and reads it with pride *Kritika Chatterjee, Special Correspondent.* She opens her bag and then places a few visiting cards in it. She then takes out a photograph of her family and places it with affection, in the corner of her station. It is a photograph of four people in the rain with the iconic India Gate in the background. That moment is very close to her heart.

With only five minutes left for the scheduled meeting, she picks up the notepad and moves towards the meeting room. Rakesh and Shivani also arrive and place their bags on their desks.

Kritika is the first one to enter the room, followed by Shivani and Rakesh.

Kritika smiles. "Hi Shivani. Hi Rakesh. I am Kritika, your new neighbor."

This must be the new girl. Smart girl. They both think.

"Hi. Good to have one more lovely neighbor." Rakesh shoots two birds with one stone.

"Hi Kritika. Nice to meet you," responds Shivani.

The door opens and Aditya enters the room.

Imagine you are a corporate veteran and have worked with all kinds of bosses. Now pick your worst boss among those. There are very good chances that Aditya will resemble that boss.

"Good morning, everyone. Let's all welcome Kritika to News 360."

"Thank you, Aditya. It's a pleasure."

"Let's hope you will not be as inefficient as your predecessor." Aditya puts an end to the pleasantries in his inimitable style.

"Let's start with the meeting. Rakesh, what is the progress on your report?"

"It's in the final editing stage. Should be ready by two o'clock."

Aditya snarls, "That will make it three hours late from your deadline."

He shifts his attention towards Shivani. "Moving on, what about you Shivani? Are you also behind on your schedule?"

I can't lie to him. She finally blurts, "Still working on my story on corruption in land acquisition for the upcoming airport. I have got some documents on dubious deals by the developer and his coterie to inflate costs. But I need at least a week more to cross verify and fine tune the story."

"It's going to be a big story. Make sure you are being extra careful."

Just when Shivani starts to feel happy that the boss cares for his team members, Aditya adds, "It's my reputation that is on the line, not yours."

"Yes, Aditya," Shivani replies sheepishly. *What an asshole!*

"Kritika, any ideas on your first story?"

Not realizing, it is a rhetorical question which doesn't warrant a response, Kritika answers, "Aditya, there was a case of suicide by a research scholar last month. I think there is a story here."

"I don't see any story!" Aditya is a pro at shooting down budding journalists with his 'humility'. *You are assigned stories, here, in this room.*

Kritika still not realizing, adds, "Off late there have

been many suicide cases in the country…"

Aditya immediately stops her. "Nobody cares! There is a story I want you to work on with Rakesh right now. I am assigning it to both of you."

After the briefing, the room disperses. Rakesh consoles Kritika, "You are lucky. Today he was soft. Welcome to News 360."

Kritika realizes it's not a team meeting but a military briefing by the Commander-in-Chief. You listen to the orders and obey. Asking questions or giving ideas is not appreciated.

Kritika reaches her station. She looks at the time in her wristwatch. *8:30 AM. It's time to call Baba.*

Dwarka
July 7, 8:30 AM

Bang. Bang Bang. There is repeated banging on the door.

"Get up you moron. It's already 8:30 AM."

There is no response. There is a bang on the door again, only louder this time. The shabby looking door has been subjected to many such bangs over a period of time. It is in such a frail state now that it might crumble any day.

"Ayush, get up. I am leaving now," Prashant shouts.

The last bang finally reaches the ears of Ayushman. He looks at the time and gets up in panic. *Not on the first day of the semester! At least this sem, I want to be on time!*

"Oh God. I shouldn't have played PUBG, so late in the night."

Ayushman rushes and opens the door with brush and toothpaste in his hand. The visitor has already left by then.

The brushing of teeth is finished in a whisker. He looks at the time. Taking a bath is no longer an option. He quickly changes into a pair of rugged blue jeans and a white color round neck t-shirt.

Salute to the man who invented the Deodorant. Must have been an Engineer. He applies the deo, picks up his bag and bike keys in a flash. Then he rushes to the hostel mess and takes a look at the breakfast.

Whoever has kept the name 'mess' is a genius!

Prashant is finishing his breakfast, he notices. *Why can't I be like him?*

He picks up two slices of bread and applies jam on them and finishes his breakfast in two bites.

Prashant comes to him and says, "You finally came."

"How do you manage to get up on time after sleeping so late?"

"If you had a *pita* like mine, you would also get up on time."

"No thanks. I am very happy with my dad."

They both laugh. They call anyone *pita* who is a *pain in the ass.*

"Thank God, mom finally went through the divorce with him. My childhood was traumatic."

"We should rush. We only have about eight minutes to reach the classroom. Damn they have introduced ALBELA (Aadhar Linked Biometric EnabLed Attendance) system from this semester. Mom, Dad will know if we are late to the class."

"What is the worry when we have your Pulsar 220F."

They run together towards it. Ayushman starts the bike

and Prashant sits on the pillion.

It's almost 9 AM by the time they reach the classroom. They are the last to punch in their attendance. Ayushman looks inside and notices Vaidehi has already saved a seat for him. Seeing him, she waves her hand.

They all have taken this elective. But Prashant soon realizes the ugly truth that every male must encounter at least once in his lifetime. *Bromance lasts only till romance starts.* He will have to sit alone. Prashant discovers that taking this elective on Ayush's insistence was a mistake.

"It was a trap. Boys are friends only till a girl is not in the picture," grumbles Prashant.

"You are a lucky dude."

"C'mon. I have been friends with her since I was in school. You know she is Deepak uncle's daughter. We are just friends."

"I know, 'just' friends." He air-quotes 'just', with his fingers. Prashant looks at Vaidehi but her eyes are on Ayushman. *Even Vaidehi and I are friends since school, but why not me?* Prashant silently goes and sits on one of the many empty chairs in the front row.

Ayushman moves towards the chair waiting for him at the back.

First love has its own intoxication.

Chapter 3
Vistāra
(Expansion)

Office, Home Minister
September 4, 9:30 AM

Mantriji and Ajay are sitting on the sofa. Manohar is dressed in a traditional white dhoti kurta. Ajay is wearing his official police uniform. They are sipping tea. This is not an official meeting but an informal interaction. Ajay senses that the minister is quite happy with the way things are shaping up. In fact, it is much better than what he had expected. Manohar rarely offers anyone, a cup of tea.

"I am very happy with the performance of your team at CIU. With such a small team, you have been able to solve every case assigned to you in record time. It is quite amazing, really!"

"Thank you, sir. I will convey your appreciation to the team."

After a brief pause, Manohar says, "I can hear a lot of whispers in the corridor and sense a growing curiosity among your peers, about how this special team is functioning so well. Yesterday, I received a congratulatory call from the Pradhan Mantriji himself. But I could sense his cautionary tone. He said it should not end up with bad publicity. Elections are just around the corner."

The look on Manohar's face is serious. The stakes were high as Manohar was also eyeing the top post of Prime Minister in the coming elections. He was now among the best performing ministers in the cabinet. Ajay realizes that the minister needed some words of reassurance.

"Sir, things are under control. I have chosen my team very carefully and all of them are highly motivated and trustworthy. They agree with our methods and understand that it is the need of the hour."

"These investigation and interrogation methods…what exactly are these? Media is speculating a lot and the word 'torture' pops up every now and then."

"Sir, the less you know, the better. This way it keeps you protected with plausible deniability."

Sensing the discomfort with the reply, he adds, "Sir, please be assured that there is no torture. The special powers are used very carefully and with absolute prudence. Sir, we may have crossed the *laxman rekha*, but I have laid down very strict internal rules to prevent any misuse. Everything is being video recorded. If this experiment is successful for another one year, we can go public. With our positive results and the public opinion in our favor, we can think of legitimizing the whole program."

Manohar seems to breathe a little easier with this assurance. "That sounds reasonable," he says, somewhat satisfied. "The public is indeed very happy and we have been able to restore their faith in the police's capabilities to solve crimes. I am sure the liberals and human rights activists will also be on our side. This could become a big election issue. Till then, ensure everything stays a secret."

"Absolutely, sir."

With his nerves settled, Manohar looks at Ajay and smiles, "So tell me, what special request do you have today?"

Ajay pulls out a file from his briefcase and pushes it towards Manohar. "Sir, it is more of a personal favor. I had told you about my nephew, Suryakant, who joined IPS even though he could have easily got into IAS or IRS or IFS."

"Yes, I remember you telling me. Very few with such high rank in UPSC join IPS."

"Sir, he had lost his father a few years back. The police could not catch the culprit. This motivated him to return to India giving up his high-paying job in the US and join the IPS. And also, in many ways, I feel that I failed him. I was busy in my own life and was never there for him."

Manohar knows where this is going. Such requests are not uncommon to him; he gets them almost on a daily basis. He puts down his glasses.

"As such in CIU, I have selected very capable, experienced and trustworthy officers. Even though Suryakant is not experienced, he is a very bright and motivated officer, right for the job. He has performed extremely well in the training. I know it may sound like I am favoring him, as he is my nephew. So, I am seeking your prior approval for recruiting him to CIU."

"Ajay, there is a big difference between training and actual field experience. It is a big favor you are asking for." Manohar knows it is not a big favor, but it is always better to make the other person feel that way.

Ajay nods and looks at Manohar. "I will be highly obliged, sir."

Hearing the words Manohar smiles and reciprocates, "I have always trusted your instincts. If you feel he will be able to fit in, you have my approval."

"Thank you for understanding, sir. I am sure he will not disappoint."

Ajay leaves the room with a sense of satisfaction. He had got what he wanted.

Nothing succeeds like success.

Chapter 4

SAMBANDHA (RELATION)

Residence, Karol Bagh
September 5, 6 AM

"Om Namoh Ganpate Vasudevaya. Om Namoh Ganpate Vasudevaya. Om Namoh Gan..."

Sudarshan Chatterjee effortlessly picks himself up from sleep and completes the sacred mantra, "...pate Vasudevaya." He has never needed an alarm to wake up.

Shruti is still asleep by his side. A brief smile lights up his aging face. Sudarshan moves to open the curtains of his room and immerses himself in the golden gaze of the rising sun. He folds his hands and prays to the Sun god, the one god that is *Pratyaksh*. Shruti is unmoved by the sunrays lighting up the room. Sudarshan goes back to the bed and picks up his cell phone kept on the side table. He does not like to be disturbed while sleeping, so the phone is always put on silent mode before going to bed. He experiences a sense of relief on seeing no new messages or missed calls. Especially today.

His daily routine commences. The walk to the kitchen is slow. There is a bottle kept near the gas stove. He picks up the bottle of water and gulps it down. Sudarshan then moves to the bathroom and quickly takes a cold shower.

Shruti is still asleep. He likes it this way as it helps him to follow his specific morning schedule. This morning solitude, allows him to meditate, recalibrate his focus, and plan his day. There are specific designated places in his house for each of these activities.

Sudarshan removes his slippers as he joins his hands and walks into the small temple in the house, to offer prayers. The temple has an assemblage of statues and photos, carefully chosen from the crores of Gods and Goddesses in India. The Shivalinga is from Rameshwaram, Sita-Rama Statue from Bhadrachalam, the Ganpati statue from Mumbai's Siddhivinayak temple, Hanuman photo from Salasar Balaji and Saraswati statue from Ancient Sharada Peeth in Pakistan occupied Kashmir (PoK), one of the oldest surviving temples of the Goddess.

Each God and Goddess has its specific relevance to Sudarshan and Shruti. Shiva is the destroyer of evil and ego. Rama, Vishnu's avatar, is a hermit king and Sita, an ideal woman, a devoted wife and symbol of Mother Earth - together they form the perfect pair. Lord Ganesha wrote the epic Mahābhārata, composed by Rishi Vyasa. Goddess Saraswati is the possessor of knowledge. It is said that Lord Hanuman, the *Gyangun Saagar* wrote a beautiful Ramayana.

It was so beautiful that on reading it, Valmiki cried fearing that no one will ever read his version now. So, Hanuman destroyed his version symbolizing that he never sought any recognition for his work. He is, thus, an epitome of pure devotion.

Sudarshan sits before these deities and meditates here every day.

He then goes to his study. Unlike most studies, this study is not a part of the main house. Sudarshan has got it made in his garden, encircling a banyan tree, the only surviving one in the hustle and bustle of this posh locality. The banyan tree has always been revered and has been the site of learning and teaching in ancient Indian culture. Sudarshan gave the respect, this old wisdom tree fittingly deserved. The study, housed more than five hundred titles spanning religion, spirituality, yoga, quantum physics, chemistry, biology and human psychology.

As he sits under the banyan tree in his study, Sudarshan seeks inspiration from the Almighty.

ll Aum Shreem Bhreem Saraswathaye Namaha ll

Sudarshan then picks up a thick ragged diary. The diary has an engraving in the center. He smiles and then starts writing in it.

As he comes out of his study, Sudarshan realizes that Shruti has also woken up and she is gazing at him from the window of their room. He walks straight to the room and holds Shruti from behind and kisses her gently on the neck. The world seems so perfect in that moment. They both know how lucky they are to have found each other.

Meanwhile, Radhey, their domestic servant, has kept breakfast ready along with the day's newspaper on the terrace. They both go together to the terrace. Sudarshan never eats without taking a bath and offering morning prayers. But Shruti does not follow such rules or schedules. The relationship is so complete that both accept each other's ways without making any effort to change the other.

Sudarshan quickly finishes his breakfast. There is a sense of urgency today. He has an important meeting with the management of his company. Financial matters have never interested him but to be able to make a difference to the world, he understands the importance of money.

Knowing that this is the time when Sudarshan normally plans for his day, Shruti asks, "What time is the meeting?"

"The meeting of the Board is at 11 AM. Deepak is getting very nervous about the financial health of the company. He feels that the business is not expanding as expected and our growth has been quite slow."

"Well, you can't blame him for feeling this way."

"I know he has the company's best interests at heart. But not everything is about money. He fails to see the bigger picture."

"Will Indu also be there in the meeting?"

"Yes, she will be. Her support is crucial. We go way back... to college. She understands how I feel about these expansion plans."

Sudarshan starts to read the newspaper, quickly glancing through the important news. He has never been a sports enthusiast or a financial expert or a person with any political leaning, so very few news items interest him.

Suddenly, his cell phone phone rings. *It's 8:30 AM.*

It must be Kritika. He affectionately waits for her call every morning. Elated, he answers the call.

"Good morning, Baba."

"Good morning, beta. How is your throat?"

Kritika hadn't been well for nearly a week now. The unexpected shower a few days back, coupled with her two-minute dance in the rain, thinking this would be the last shower for the season, had left her with painful tonsils and a running nose. She hides all that from her father, "It's better now."

"Your voice doesn't seem to be normal. Are you doing the salt-water gargles and steam with Karvol plus capsules regularly?"

She lies to avoid another long lecture from Sudarshan, "Yes, Baba. Exactly the way you told me."

"Good."

Longer the conversation with Baba, higher are the chances of many such uncomfortable questions. She decides to end it with, "Give the phone to Mumma."

Sudarshan hands the phone over to Shruti. "How are you Kriti?"

"I am doing good, Mumma. I need your input on my special report on pressure on research scholars in universities and colleges. After nearly two months of efforts, I could convince my boss to do this story. I am emailing it to you. Please look at it quickly and let me know."

Shruti is a Master of Arts in English literature apart from being an accomplished oil painter. She had quit her teaching job a couple of years back on health grounds. "Sure, beta. I will call you back within an hour, after Sudarshan leaves for office."

She adds, "You are coming home today *na*? You did not come last weekend. Even Ayush missed coming home last weekend." Kritika had moved out around five months back, as commuting from Noida to Karol Bagh daily was getting difficult. Daughters are more like friends to their mothers and Shruti misses her.

"My boss Adi didn't let me go last weekend. He is a very tough boss. But I will definitely come in the late evening today."

Shruti is delighted to hear this. Enthusiastically, she says, "Ok, beta."

"Call me back with the inputs, Mumma. Say bye to Baba."

"Yes, beta. Bye."

The call gets disconnected. Sudarshan is all smiles. "Shruti, it's been a while since all of us have gone out together."

"Yes, even I am eagerly waiting for some family time. Let's plan out a vacation soon."

"Soon, looks difficult. Business needs my attention. Maybe during Ayush's winter holidays, we can plan a family vacation to Europe."

"Yeah, I understand." She looks at the time in the cell. "You better get ready to leave for the meeting."

The thought of the meeting returns to Sudarshan as he gets ready to leave.

Just as Sudarshan sits in his car, Shruti gets a call on her phone.

It is Deepak.

❖ ❖ ❖

Chapter 5
SARP
(THE "CIU")

Headquarters, CIU
Location Undisclosed

September 5, 10:45 AM

A confident looking man in his late twenties, dressed in khaki (police uniform), removes his sunglasses and looks at the building. He has a good height and an average build. His light brown complexion, short hair and clean-shaven face makes him look much younger than a man of his age. Before entering, the man touches his heart with a closed fist. It's a reminder of the promise, the one he seeks to fulfil.

By a mere look at it, it is difficult to ascertain that it is a government building. There is no board on it. The only giveaway is an *Ashoka* emblem on the glass doors. The building has a black glass facade through which one can't really see anything. He pushes the door and steps inside. The security guard at the reception stops him and asks him to show his ID and explain the purpose of his visit. Even regular policemen are not allowed in this building without proper authorization and have to mandatorily show their IDs.

The man patiently starts to reach for his wallet to take out his ID-card, when the security guard reads the name on his badge, *Suryakant Singh, IPS*. The security guard stands up and gives a salute, "Jai Hind, sir. Sorry sir, I did not recognize you."

"That's alright. You are just doing your duty." Suryakant smiles.

The security had already been instructed to escort Suryakant to the Chief's office. He hurriedly accompanies Suryakant to the elevator and as the door opens, the security guard tells the elevator operator, "Take Saahab to the second floor immediately."

The elevator opens on the second floor. The man at the entrance of the glass door has already been informed by the reception. He stands up. "Jai Hind, sir. Please follow me." The man at the door swipes his ID card on the card reader. The door gets unlocked.

"Sir, please go to room no. 201 at the end of the left corridor. Chief sir is expecting you."

Suryakant takes a slow walk through the corridor looking at the various rooms and the staff working in the open cubicles. He reads IR-2 on one door and wonders what it means. *May be Interrogation Room No 2.* He reaches the door where 201 is written on the top and 'AJAY RAJ

SINGH, Chief, Crime Investigation Unit' at the center.

A peon outside the door asks for the name of the visitor.

The peon then goes into the room and the door closes. Suryakant looks at the CCTV camera on the top of the door looking directly at him. He looks at the left of the room and reads 'VIKRAM RATHOD, Special Investigator - 1' and 'ARIF KHAN, Special Investigator - 2'. He looks to the right and sees the name 'SURYAKANT SINGH, Special Investigator - 3', on one of the rooms. He is pleasantly surprised to see his name already there.

After about ten seconds, the peon comes out and says, "Sir, you can go inside." He keeps the door open to let Suryakant enter the room.

Chief's Cabin, CIU
September 5, 11:08 AM

There is an imposing golden Ashoka Emblem with the national motto *Satyamev Jayate*, right in the center of the wall behind the Chief. There are two flags on the side of the emblem. One, the National Flag and the other, the Service Flag of the IPS. There are four telephones and a Mac desktop on his table. There are two TV screens, diametrically opposite to the Chief, one relaying CCTV footage of various places at the CIU and the other telecasting the news. Both the TVs are on mute. A big bookshelf with numerous thick and heavy books occupies the left half of the room. On the right side of the wall, there are photographs of Mahatma Gandhi and Sardar Patel along with a map of Delhi city between them.

Suryakant's eyes fall on the graceful golden name

plate on the table which reads, Ajay Raj Singh, IPS, Chief, CIU. He gives a salute, "Jai Hind, sir. IPS Suryakant Singh reporting for duty."

Ajay reciprocates, "Jai Hind. Welcome to CIU, Suryakant. Please be seated."

Suryakant takes the chair on the left and sits with both his hands on his lap.

Ajay smiles and says, "It is good to have you at the CIU."

"Sir, the privilege is all mine. I hope I have earned it. I was quite startled to find that I am posted to CIU. Haven't heard much about CIU. Nothing was told to us during the training."

Ajay had expected such a reaction. He had recruited Suryakant without even asking him. Such favors, that too so early in one's career, leave a permanent mark. Nothing is forgotten in Government. Suryakant has already been labelled as the one with a Godfather in the service. And it is this label that will always travel faster than his achievements. Ajay knew all this, but he nevertheless decided to do it. He did not see a better option.

"It is a newly formed elite unit for crime investigation with special powers. CIU directly reports to the Home Minister. It is assigned sensitive and high-profile crime cases when the regular police investigation is not able to crack the case. You can understand the pressure we work under. The expectation from CIU is very high."

Suryakant listens to each word carefully.

Ajay continues, "And regarding your selection, it was decided to pick a suitable candidate directly from NPA. Right

[1] NPA stands for National Police Academy at Hyderabad where young entrants to the IPS are trained. It conducts nearly two years of rigorous training.

before the system corrupts or renders them spineless. There is a joke in bureaucracy that with every passing year, you lose one disc in the spine, making you a perfect bureaucrat in twenty-three years." He gives a small laugh.

Suryakant gives a faint smile. *I will be different,* he says to himself.

"As you were number one in the civil list and had scored quite well in academy, you were the unanimous choice. It had nothing to do with you being my nephew. The Home Minister himself approved your selection looking at your profile." The civil list is like a Bhagwad Gita in bureaucracy. It is prepared on the basis of one's rank in the UPSC exam and defines the seniority. The rank seals your fate. If a decision to select someone for a post is to be made, just follow the civil list and nobody is likely to question it. Everyone accepts an unfair sounding practice, as fair.

Suryakant feels a bit relieved hearing these words. "Sir, what are the special powers you mentioned?"

Ajay thinks to himself. *He is indeed smart.* "As you must have already noticed, your room is ready. CIU at present has only three units, all of which directly report to me. Your designation will be Special Investigator (SI) of Unit-3. There are two inspectors and six constables in each Unit. I will introduce you to the other units and slowly you will come to know about everything including the special powers."

Suryakant starts wondering, *"Special" unit... "Special" powers... Why is there so much secrecy?*

Ajay presses the bell under his table. The peon sitting outside, enters the room, "Yes, sir."

"Please call Vikram and Khan. And get four cups of tea."

"Yes, sir." The peon quietly leaves the room.

"Suryakant, how many lions are there in the Ashoka Emblem?"

Is this a trick question? Suryakant wonders. He carefully considers and answers, "Four sir."

"How many lions do you see on the Emblem behind me?"

He looks at it and answers, "Three sir."

"Where is the fourth one?"

Suryakant wonders what kind of question that is. It's obviously a 2-D photograph, so the fourth one is hidden.

Ajay knows the dilemma in the mind of Suryakant. He has seen many with such a face over the years.

"The Fourth Lion is the one sitting on the chair, Suryakant. Always remember that."

Suryakant's face beams with pride. The moment is interrupted with a knock on the door.

"Come in."

Both Vikram Rathod and Arif Khan enter the room and give salute in tandem, "Jai Hind, sir."

Suryakant turns and takes a look at them. They both appear to be in late thirties but with strong muscular builds. They are clean shaven, short haired and have lip-sized moustaches. Arif is fairer in complexion compared to Vikram but Vikram is taller than Arif. Vikram is in uniform but Arif is in plain clothes. That is all the difference he can notice at first sight. *Intimidating officers.*

"Please take your seats, officers."

They both take the remaining two seats in front of the table.

"Meet Suryakant Singh. He will be heading Unit-3 here."

They both nod and give a soft smile but none of them look at Suryakant. It appears that they are not convinced with the recruitment of an officer, who has no field experience, into the CIU. They have read the dossier about him. His relationship with the Chief is known to them. Years of experience have taught them to let the silence do the talking in such situations.

In the meantime, tea is served by the peon.

"Suryakant, you will be working under Rathod till you are ready. This will be more like an on-the-job training. I expect you to be ready to handle a case independently, pretty soon."

The words lighten up the tense face of Suryakant, as he nods.

"There is just one rule - complete secrecy in what we do. Whatever happens here, remains within the four corners of this office. The world outside just sees our results, not how we get them. I hope I have made myself clear."

"Yes, sir."

"And do remember the motto of CIU is *Satya. Nyaya. Nānṛtam.*"

Suryakant understands what *Satya* and *Nyaya* means but he wonders what is *Nānṛtam.*

Ajay adds, "Wondering what *Nānṛtam* means?"

"Yes, sir."

"It means truth alone leads to justice, not falsehood. At CIU, our special powers are to ensure that we remove the 'lies' from the 'truth', to get to the actual truth. We do what no one else does - solve each case and don't let falsehood get away."

Suryakant gives a confused smile.

"Any further questions you have, will be answered by him." Ajay moves his gaze towards Rathod. "Over to you Rathod."

"Yes, sir."

"And all can proceed now."

They all get up even though they have taken only two sips of tea. They give salutations and leave the room. Arif proceeds to his room without saying a word. Suryakant follows Vikram to his office in silence.

SI-1, CIU
September 5, 11:20 AM

The room is nearly three-fourths the size of the Chief's room and it has all the usual décor except one. There is no TV screen relaying CCTV footage. That privilege is only with the Chief. Vikram swiftly moves and sits on the chair. "Please be seated, Suryakant."

Suryakant sits on the chair. His back is straight and his eyes are looking directly into Vikram's eyes.

"I have read your file. You profile is impressive. You have done well at NPA as well."

"Thank you, sir."

"Please call me Vikram. There is no seniority here in CIU. We all are equal."

"Yes, sir. I mean Vikram sir." He knows 'sir' is not optional, even when it's told to be. A senior is always addressed as 'sir'. This is Bureaucracy 101.

"So, do you have any questions?"

"What are the special powers of CIU?"

"We have our own lab and our own interrogation techniques. Rest is all about your intellect and instincts. The best way to learn is to work on a live case." He pushes a file marked "Case No. 18" towards Suryakant.

"A case has been received this morning after police investigation made no progress. Wife of a well-known cardiologist Dr. Sumit Mehta is missing for the past three days. The file has everything that has so far been gathered by the police. Go through it and let us meet again in an hour."

The conversation had ended rather quickly. Suryakant picks up the file and leaves the room after giving salutations.

SI-3, CIU
September 5, 11:35 AM

Suryakant enters his room feeling an unusual pressure. The file weighed only a few hundred grams, but it felt like a five-kilogram dumbbell. He did not expect to get a case on his very first day. He immediately goes and sits on the chair. There is no time to look around his room or feel the comfort of the chair. He starts turning the pages of the file.

The file contained the FIR about the missing person, Mrs. Suman Mehta, aged 38 years. It mentioned that she is missing since last three days. She left her home at around 7 AM and never returned after her aerobics class, which ended at 8:30 AM. The car she used to drive to the class was also missing. In the evening, her husband Dr. Sumit Mehta reported her "missing" to the police after her phone was not reachable for hours and she did not return home.

No mention of any ransom call till now, he wonders.

The file had the statements of Dr. Sumit Mehta, his son, the home servant, aerobics instructor, the security guard at the gym and a few of her friends and neighbors. The call data records (CDRs) of Mrs. Suman Mehta and all the other potential suspects were kept in the file. Few CCTV footages and the statements of her bank accounts and credit cards were also enclosed.

The CDR of Mrs. Suman Mehta showed that the last call was made to Dr. Sumit Mehta at around 8 PM, the night before she went missing. There were no calls after that. Unfortunately missed calls are not reported in the CDR. No CCTV footage of the home was available even though it was installed. *It was not working for the last one month! That's surprising!* Suryakant thinks to himself.

He looks at the wall clock and 45 minutes had already passed. The pressure starts to build on him. The clock is ticking very rapidly. His last memory of the clock ticking so rapidly was of his UPSC general studies paper. He is unable to notice anything out of the ordinary nor is able to ascertain any potential leads which have not already been explored by the police.

The alibi of Dr. Sumit Mehta looks solid. He left home early and reached the hospital at around 8:30 AM for a surgery which lasted for nearly four hours. After coming out of surgery he tried calling his wife several times but the phone was not reachable. The aerobics instructor and security guard confirmed that Mrs. Suman Mehta left around 8:30 AM as usual. There was nobody with her in the car. They had seen her leave, driving the car. The nearby CCTV footage confirmed the same. The car had not been found so far. There had been no transaction reported in the bank statement or the credit card statement in the last one week. *Maybe she drove somewhere to stay alone and paid in cash.*

There was absolutely no lead. The only thing he could think of was to track the car through the CCTV footage at traffic signals, shops and ATMs. But it would be practically impossible to collect all the footage and go through them. They did not have any such access. Maybe **R&AW** or Intelligence Bureau (**IB**) would have them, but not **CIU**.

Dr. Sumit Mehta suspected it to be a kidnapping case. But no ransom call had been received till now. Normally, they are received within the first 24 hours. If no ransom is communicated within 24 hours, it is likely to be a murder investigation.

But again, no dead body was found or reported by anyone. He again starts going through the file from the beginning, looking for something to say to Vikram. Realization dawns upon him that there is a lot of difference between case studies he did at NPA and an actual live case. As he looks at the time on the wall clock, he realizes that it is less than five minutes to his appointment.

His heart starts beating even more rapidly.

Chapter 6

KUBER (WEALTH)

SSKA Office, Mayapuri
September 5, 10 AM

The office of SSKA Private Limited is in a four-storied building at the industrial area in Mayapuri. The company has occupied the top three floors in the building. The ground floor is rented to ICICI bank. The building appears old but is in a relatively good condition compared to the neighborhood.

Deepak Agarwal, Chartered Accountant and Chief Financial Officer (CFO) of the company, is in his room giving final touches to the presentation for the AGM at 11 AM. He is not very enthused with what he is seeing. *Things can be so much better without him.* The landline rings and breaks Deepak's thoughts.

"Good morning, sir, this is Sachin Shukla calling from Nexis bank - relationship Manager for SSKA."

Deepak knows any call from the bank is bad news. The company has missed payment of EMI on the term loan.

"Hi Sachin, how are you? How can I help you?"

"Sir, I regret to inform you that you have defaulted on the repayment of your term loan. You credit limits have already been reduced last month. I am afraid that we will have to start taking coercive steps."

"I am sorry, Sachin. We need some more time. Our relationship with your bank goes back a decade. This is a rough time for us but we are expecting a turnaround soon."

"You will have to come down this week and explain to us this turnaround plan."

"I will fix up a meeting. Thanks, Sachin." Deepak hangs up the phone in a pensive mood. He looks at the photo of his daughter Vaidehi on his desk for a while. Eight years ago, when he joined the company, it looked like an excellent opportunity. *We indeed need a turnaround. Only Indu can put some sense into him. Today's meeting is an important one.* Deepak picks up his laptop and walks into her room.

Indu is working on her desktop checking her inbox for emails. She is old styled and prefers a desktop to a laptop.

"Indu, I need your support today in the AGM. This company cannot be made a victim of his whims and fantasies."

Indu listens and gives no response.

"I have a proposal. If it comes from your mouth, he might accept it."

September 5, 11 AM

Sudarshan reaches the conference room on the second floor of the office building. It's a small room but is well lit with sunlight. Through the glass door, he sees Deepak, sitting in his typical white shirt, black suit with a black tie. He has his usual tense face with his eyes staring into the laptop through his glasses. Indu Mehra, his long-time friend and co-founder, is sitting opposite to him. She is wearing a light green silk saree and looks relaxed. Tanya Verma, company secretary, is also seated at the table. The silence of the room is deafening.

Sudarshan moves and sits on the central chair of the round table. There is an exchange of smiles between him and Indu. Deepak is lost in his world of numbers. He does not seem to have noticed that Sudarshan has entered and is already seated.

Sudarshan clears his throat and makes a sound, "Ahem." But Deepak is still unmoved.

Indu tries to break Deepak's spell, "Good morning, Sudarshan." This brings Deepak back from the world of numbers and to the present reality of the room. Deepak is a bit embarrassed.

"Good morning, to the Board," Deepak starts the meeting. "The agenda for today's meeting is to present the annual results for the last financial year. The discussion will also be on the financial health of the company and the measures required to improve it." The strain and unhappiness in his voice can be easily felt.

Deepak presses a button on his laptop and the PowerPoint presentation starts on the projector. "This graph shows total revenues of the last five years. After a good growth in the first two years, there is stagnancy in last three years." He presses the button again and the next slide appears.

"This is the position of our expenditure." Without elaborating this slide, he quickly moves to the next one. "This summarizes the first two slides. It gives the position of the Profit & Loss account. We have not been able to reach the break-even point. Our gestation period for the new product has already been over shot by two years from what we had expected."

He continues, "Our revenue sources are limited. We don't seem to be going anywhere. We need money… I think it's time we start looking for funding from some potential investors."

Indu listens quietly. Sudarshan immediately reverts, "That's not an option. This company will remain in our hands." The figures and numbers have not been able to unnerve Sudarshan. His reply is calm and composed. Sudarshan founded this company eight years ago to live a dream. He was earlier a professor in a college, before leaving the teaching profession, to start something of his own. As a founder and the brain behind the company, nobody has much of a say over what he decided.

Deepak tries to argue, "We have already defaulted on our term loan and our credit limits have already been reduced. We won't be able to survive for more than six months with our current finances. We will be unable to pay salaries and other expenses. I got a call from the bank today, they want us to come up with a turnaround plan, otherwise they might take coercive steps."

"We have to be patient. If required, I will introduce

more capital. I am ready to sell or mortgage my house."

Deepak can't believe what Sudarshan had just said. "Sudarshan, we are already in heavy debt. You have spent nearly all of yours and even Shruti's savings. The house is in Shruti's name, it's her ancestral home. Have you even spoken with her?"

"I can get her to do it."

"The house is the only asset left with you. Getting investors is not such a bad option. You will still have managing control," Indu interjects.

"But I want only persons I completely trust entering this room. You both are like my family. We have been together and will get through this rough phase."

There is pin drop silence in the room. Sudarshan has spoken in such a stern voice that it has closed the scope for any further discussion on getting new investors. Deepak nods his head and starts biting the nail of his thumb. He is trying his best to maintain his composure.

Indu is the mediator between the two. This role fits her personality and she has been doing it for a long time now. She intervenes, "But we can explore expanding our clientele and maybe charging a bit more for our products."

Sudarshan is not as harsh in his reply as earlier, "I know you both may disagree, but I do not wish this company to become a Fortune 500 company but we will definitely be in the list of Top 100 companies that changed the world. Create art, don't worry about how it is perceived." With a brief pause, he continues, "Yes. Expanding our clientele is an option but I am against charging more for our products."

Indu responds in her mild voice and with a smile, "At least we agree on something. We can start looking to expand our clientele for now."

Deepak's thumb is finally freed from his teeth. His hand comes down and rests on the table. Deepak nods in agreement, "I will start talking with potential clients."

Deepak signals Indu with his eyes. Indu's gaze moves from Deepak to Sudarshan, "We can also think of demerging our product under development into a new company. This way the books of SSKA will reflect earnings only from our successful products which are our cash cows. Banks will also find our books more palatable this way." It is Deepak's plan to ensure that loss-making products die a natural death in the newly demerged company.

Deepak nods his head in agreement. "Yes, that's a good idea."

Sudarshan relents as this proposal has come from Indu, "I see no harm with the proposal."

It worked. Deepak is delighted.

"I will send the minutes of the Board meeting within an hour for signature."

Sudarshan thanks all of them with handshakes. He gets up and leaves the room. Tanya follows him. Deepak closes his laptop and starts to pick it up. Indu gets up and starts to move towards the door. Deepak stops her, "Do you really understand him? Is he really ready to sell his house?"

Indu knows Sudarshan very well. She had joined the company at his insistence. They both have been a good team and have led the company well in its formative years. "He is easy to understand if you remove money as one of the parameters to judge him. His approach is vastly different, but he is essential to this company."

"I hope someday he understands Chanakya's wisdom *Kosh Mulo Dand.* Finance is the root of a company. He is a man of ideas; he should leave finances to experts. Without finance whatever we are trying to achieve, will get lost sooner or later."

Indu does not say anything.

Deepak takes a step closer to Indu and then slowly whispers, "How is the progress on what we had discussed?"

Indu gets a bit nervous, "I am working on it, but haven't got any breakthrough yet."

Deepak holds her hand and whispers, "This can be a goldmine. But it needs to be a secret. He cannot get to know anything about it. This is for the future of our children."

We can get rid of him if this works.

September 5, 11:45 AM

Sudarshan too is returning to his room with the thoughts of the meeting still troubling his mind. *The banks have asked us to come up with a plan.*

Priya Mehta, his secretary, for the last five years, gets up from the chair. "How was the meeting sir?"

"It went better than I had anticipated," he smiles.

Priya wonders whether it is the right time to speak. But a secretary is also supposed to be the eyes and ears of the boss in the company. Staying true to her job, she gathers courage and says, "I think I should tell you. There is a rumor going around in the office, that the company has defaulted on its loans. The future of the company is uncertain."

"Who said that?"

"As I said, it's a rumor in the office, sir."

"There is no problem. We discussed it in the AGM and will find a solution. The company is in good hands." He barges into his room. Priya has never seen Sudarshan so tense.

The Padma Shri is hanging on the wall and staring down at Sudarshan.

I won't let anything happen to this company, no matter what.

Chapter 7

SŪCHĪ
(THE LIST)

SI-1, CIU
September 5, 12:30 PM

Suryakant knocks on the door and opens it slightly.

"Come in," says a deep voice. Suryakant enters the room. File of Case No. 18 is in his hand. His unquiet mind can be easily seen on his face.

"Please sit down."

Suryakant softly sits with his head down. He pushes the file towards Vikram.

"So, what is your opinion. How should we proceed?"

"I don't have many ideas Vikram sir. The disappearance of Mrs. Suman Mehta is indeed very mysterious. On the basis of what is in the file, I don't know what to say."

This is the answer Vikram expected from an honest investigator. He likes the way Suryakant does not try to show-off with an unnecessary urge to impress, instead he is brave enough to admit that he does not have any leads. Vikram also has a soft corner for Suryakant as they both are graduates from the prestigious IIT.

Impressed by his honesty, he lets go of his officious pretensions and chooses to mentor him. "First rule of investigation - start referring to the person under investigation as "victim" and not by their names. This way you try to remove your personal opinions and judgements from clouding the investigation. You will not get attached to the victim or try to sympathize with her. Next, you prepare a list of suspects in order of probabilities. Use your gut feeling to your advantage. You know, first instincts normally turn out to be right unless the criminal is very smart.

Second rule of investigation - never trust the statements given by the witnesses and the suspects. Try to find contradictions. What people tell you, is what they want you to know or think, which is, mostly to mislead you. Never miss the truth by running from one lie to another.

Third rule - try to cull out the facts. Remove ambiguities. An investigator must look beyond the obvious. For that you need to separate hard facts from opinions and assumptions."

Suryakant is listening patiently and intently. He likes the way Vikram is guiding him which he really had not expected. The first meeting gave him an impression that he is a tough and an arrogant superior. But in the second meeting he was turning out to be a gentle and an understanding teacher.

"Who should be our suspect number one?"

Suryakant is ready with an answer to this question, "It

should be the husband."

"Well that will be the case in 8 out of 10 cases. But what makes you think so?" Vikram knew, more than determining the suspect, the reason for doing so, was more important. This when followed and done correctly, will tell how good an investigator, Suryakant will ultimately turn out to be.

"The CDR for the phone number of Dr. Mehta shows that the cell phone was changed just a week before." *Good observation*, Vikram thinks. Suryakant continues, "It is mentioned in the report by IT that the WhatsApp had very few conversations. Further, CCTV at home was not working for nearly a month and no one did anything to fix it."

Vikram is used to getting the most obvious answer from his other junior colleagues that by virtue of being the Husband, he should be the Suspect No. 1. But with Suryakant, more than the answer, Vikram is pleased with the reasoning which he has given.

"Very well put. Who should be suspect number two?"

Suryakant remains quiet and continues to think. *Which name should I pick? The gym instructor or home servant or...*

"The phone log of the victim never lies. It tells you more than any other statement. It is an evidence which cannot be manipulated or twisted."

Suryakant has a photographic memory. Normally, it is quite easy to remember the irrelevant and forget the relevant. But Suryakant remembers everything, even the relevant. Even in his college and school days, he was famous as a 'Maggu' (one who can memorize everything). Many times, he remembered the answers after he had seen them just once. Thus, here also there was no need for Suryakant to turn pages and locate the phone log analysis report of the victim.

"She had the maximum number of calls with her husband and then with her son, which is what one should expect," he answers effortlessly.

Vikram is mighty impressed. "Think deeper. See with whom she had the maximum duration of call and not just the number of calls."

The maximum duration of call is with… "It's with the neighbor."

"Is that an expected thing?"

"No, sir. That's not normal." Suryakant feels bad about how he missed it.

"Further, they call each other between 8 AM to 9 AM, which may be normally after Dr. Mehta leaves home. But there is no call on the day she was kidnapped. Shouldn't that make him as our suspect number 2."

"Quite right, sir."

Vikram now asks, "What about suspect number 3?"

Suryakant can't believe that Vikram is continuing with this discussion. *Are two initial suspects not enough to start with. Why do we need a third suspect?*

"Hmm…Do we really need to have a third suspect sir?"

Vikram smiles. "This is the difference between CIU investigation and police investigation. We solve cases within hours. But for that we need to collect evidence and have all our suspects in order. Then we can question them and unriddle the mystery."

How is that even possible? We will question them and solve the case! This looks like a newcomer's trick being played, to make me look like a fool.

"Don't look so puzzled. It's not a newcomer's trick." Vikram says, as if he has read Suryakant's mind.

"It has to be either the gym instructor or the house servant."

"Give me one name. We need to have a suspect priority list. There can't be two names at the same place."

Suryakant randomly picks, "The gym instructor. He is the last one who had seen the victim."

"Good. Even I would have thought so," Vikram responds.

"Anyone else you want to put on the list?"

"Sir, even the house servant is a potential suspect. His behavior is suspicious. He prepares the breakfast. When the victim does not return from the aerobics class, he doesn't do anything. Neither he tries to call the victim or the husband. This is something which is suspicious."

Vikram sees the logic. *Even I did not think of that.* "Good observation. So, we have an initial list of four suspects - husband, friend, gym instructor and home servant." He writes the names in serial order on a paper and keeps it in his pocket.

"We already have the husband in IR-1, the friend in IR-2 and the gym instructor in IR-3." Vikram presses the bell.

Inspector Shekhar walks in. "Yes, sir."

"Shekhar, get the home servant Badrinath picked up and bring him to IR-4."

"Right, sir." Shekhar leaves immediately. A seasoned subordinate always knows his bosses' ways.

Suryakant gathers some courage for asking a trivial question, "Does IR means Investigation Room or Interrogation Room?"

Vikram smiles. "Yes, it's Interrogation Room. Here we will question the suspects and try to solve the case." With the list in hand, he asks, "Are you ready?"

"Yes, sir."

Vikram picks up the landline phone and dials a code. "We are going in."

Chapter 8

Saṃyoga (Together)

The door bell rings. Radhey comes out of the kitchen and goes to open the door. "Bitiya (daughter)!" He immediately moves to take the bag from Kritika.

"Radhey chacha (uncle), I can manage this small bag." But Radhey takes it anyways. "Where is everybody?" she asks.

"Sir comes around 6:30. Madam and Ayush beta have gone out to the market. They must be coming back soon."

"Ohh." She goes inside, sits on the sofa and takes out her cell phone. *Should I call Mumma?* But then she decides not to.

Radhey comes with a glass of water.

"Thanks."

Kritika takes two small sips and keeps the glass on the table.

"Madam, tea or coffee. Any snack you want me to make?"

"Coffee and if I can have your pakodas Radhey chacha that will be great."

"Ji bitiya." *Yes, daughter.* A smiling Radhey walks to the kitchen.

Her eyes move to the wall clock, it is nearly 5:30 pm. She reaches for the remote, turns on the TV and presses 5 8 8 on the remote. "News 360" channel appears. It is time for her story, the one she has been working on for the last two weeks, to be telecasted.

We now take you to a special story by Ms. Kritika Chatterjee, our special correspondent reporting from New Delhi ...

She says to herself - *one day I will also be on TV, commanding my own segment.* As the story ends, the doorbell rings. She rushes to open the door. It is Shruti and Ayush. She hugs both of them.

"You are late. You missed my story on the TV."

"Ohh! Why didn't you tell us before? When will it come again?"

"I wanted it to be a surprise for you all. Now it will come again at 11:30 at night."

"When is Baba coming?"

"He will leave the office at around 6:30, at his normal time and will reach by 7. If you had told him, he would have come early."

They enter the house and make themselves comfortable on the sofa. Ayushman is busy on his phone.

"Ayush, why are you so silent? You have been constantly on the phone since you entered. Put that thing down." Ayushman keeps the phone down as if he has been caught.

"With whom are you busy WhatsApping? Is that your girlfriend?" Kritika fires an arrow in the dark on a shy and introvert Ayushman.

"Nooooh. She is just a college friend…My…My mid-semester exam results are expected anytime." *Shit I said 'she'. Now they know.* Ayushman is hoping that they don't ask further questions about this college *friend,* Vaidehi Agarwal, whom he has recently started dating.

"Oooooh." Kritika teases Ayushman. The arrow stuck.

Ayushman is already feeling awkward, when out of nowhere, Shruti says something even more unexpected, "What is her name?" Caught totally off-guard by the remark, he utters, "What?"

Both Shruti and Kritika keep staring with their inquisitive eyes. They want a name. Ayushman realizes that there is no escape now. He relents, "Vaidehi."

They all know who Vaidehi is. Shruti and Kritika smile, in approval. Shruti makes another surprise attack, "Why don't you invite her for dinner tonight?"

"What?" Ayushman wears a puzzled look, but is happy within. *Mumma knows what I want.* "Are you serious Mumma?"

"Yes, invite her. She lives nearby."

With a lot of smiles and blushes, he says, "I will check

with her, if she is available."

"Where had you both gone?" Kritika shifts to Shruti without digging further, so it doesn't feel more awkward.

Ayushman starts to reply, "We went to…" Shruti intervenes, "We went to the market for some shopping." Shruti and Ayushman share a look.

"What did you buy?" Kritika asks.

Shruti replies, "Just bought two pairs of jeans for him. But we had to leave them for alteration. Will get them tomorrow." Radhey walks in with three cups of coffee and three plates of pakodas. He starts to serve each one of them. Kritika quickly grabs the pakodas and finishes them in a jiffy. "I should go and freshen up."

"Yes, Sudarshan should be home by then. We will have a family dinner tonight. I will have your favorite dishes cooked by then."

Kritika leaves. Ayushman and Shruti share a relieved look.

She can't know.

September 5, 7:10 PM

The doorbell rings. Sudarshan is at the door. Shruti comes and opens the door. "How was your day?"

"The usual. Nothing exciting."

"Well, I know what will cheer you up."

Kritika just walks in. Sudarshan smiles as if all the worries of the world have melted away. They both hug each other and start walking in.

"My special report was telecasted today on 'News 360'. Finally, I got some screen time."

"I knew you would do great. When do we get to watch it?"

"It was telecasted at 5:30 PM. But all of you missed it. I came to surprise you."

"When will the repeat telecast come?"

She knows Baba sleeps by 10 PM every day. He was an early to bed, early to rise kind. And they all have always liked it. This way they have time for late night conversations and binge-watching Netflix, with Mumma. "It will be too late for you Baba. Now it will come only at 11:30 PM. But I think it will come again at 7 in the morning."

"I won't miss that for sure," Sudarshan smiles.

"How is the company shaping up?" she touches a raw nerve. Sudarshan had thought that Kritika would fit well in the sales team at the company. But she was always a firebrand and decided to explore journalism.

"It's going well. But I won't bore you with the details. You decided not to join and instead went for journalism. Now fulfil your dreams there." The sarcasm and disappointment in his voice were obvious.

Looking at Ayush, who was still busy on his phone, he continues, "I hope at least Ayush will continue my legacy and take the company forward."

Ayushman gives a faint smile.

September 5, 8:30 PM

All five of them are sitting at the dining table and Radhey is serving food. It's a circular six-seater dining table.

Shruti folds her hands and says the words, "*Annam Parabrahma Swaroopam.*" Food is a form of the Almighty.

Sudarshan, Kritika and Ayushman repeat the words. Vaidehi pretends to murmur something. They all start eating.

"Have the results for your mid-sem exams come?" Sudarshan asks Ayushman.

"Not yet," Ayushman replies.

Sudarshan asks Vaidehi, "How were your mid-sems Beta?"

"They went well, uncle."

"I know. You have always been a bright student."

"Are you reading any new book these days?" Shruti asks Kritika to change the topic.

"I am reading Ramayana and Mahābhārata these days as you had suggested Mumma. These are quite lengthy, complex tales and they sound ridiculous at many places. For instance, how can Rāvana have ten heads."

Ayushman laughs hearing it.

Sudarshan listens patiently and lets Kritika continue. "I also have one basic problem with these stories. They always show that the reason for everything bad that happened was a woman. Had Draupadi not laughed on Duryodhan, there might have been no war! Similarly, had Sita not asked Rama to go after the golden deer, Rāvana wouldn't have been able to kidnap Sita, the war would have been avoided! All these stories are so male centric…"

Sudarshan lets her finish and then replies to her, "I think you are missing the point. These books are trying to convey various complex messages through interesting tales. You are busy questioning the cover of the book and, therefore missing the content inside. The ten heads are the imagination of the author, to symbolize that Rāvana had the knowledge or intelligence equivalent to that of ten heads. After all, he was very learned. Don't take these things literally, go deeper."

There is a mix of astonishment and curiosity in the eyes of Kritika, Ayushman and Vaidehi.

Sudarshan continues, "Try to read the message. If you ask me, it has nothing to do with women. When I look at these stories from a parent's perspective, they teach that things go wrong when parents try to control the lives of their children. When blind love for their offspring overpowers them, it has terrible consequences."

The eating stops and all begin to listen. The discussion even attracts the attention of Radhey as he forgets to serve the chapatis that he is holding in his hand.

"In Ramayana, Kaikeyi tries to make Bharata the king instead of a more deserving Rama. She was trying to do the best for her son, which any mother would. But this ends up tearing apart the family. In Mahābhārata, Dhritarashtra ignores the mistakes of his son Duryodhana, which leads to injustice and *adharma*. This resulted in an awful war. The parents have to remember; love should not be blind. *Moh* (love) for *Santaan* (child) should never take precedence over *nyaya* (justice) or *dharma.*"

Vaidehi says, "That's such a beautiful thought, uncle. I hope dad understands this. He is very possessive about me." The words make Ayushman concerned about their future together. Vaidehi has always been a topper unlike Ayushman, who struggles to even stay afloat in the middle. This is the most basic qualification a daughter's father looks for in a prospective son-in-law.

Sudarshan smiles. "I know how he is. He loves you the

most in this world."

"Wow Baba, I did not think in this way at all! Tell us more," Kritika asks.

"Another message that is conveyed through the story is to always stand by what you promise, no matter what the consequences may be. *Raghukul reet sada chali aayi, pran jaye par vachan na jaye.* Rama goes to vanvas (exile) to fulfil the promise made by his father, even though Bharata and everyone else wants him to return. But he fulfils the promise of his father.

Yudhisthira agrees to go on vanvas even after knowing that Duryodhana cheated in the game. He made a mistake by playing the game, now he must honor his word and bear its consequences. The society stands on these principles. These stories are trying to inspire us by setting these examples. The day trust is lost chaos will ensue, and we will cease to be an orderly civilized society. This is the foundation on which the society rests.

Read these stories in this manner. Don't get lost in the imagination of the author. Make your own interpretations. Every time you read, you should get a new learning. That is how these stories have survived the test of time. They are so beautiful underneath. This is our heritage, our culture."

The mood in the room remains spiritually enlightened for the rest of the evening.

Chapter 9

Astra
(Weapon)

IR-1, CIU
September 5, 1:15 PM

Vikram swipes his card on the door. Suryakant follows him. He notices that CCTV cameras are there at every possible place.

The room has one more door and a big glass window. It is just like a holding room he had seen in the English movies. The suspect number one is sitting on the chair. The suspect doesn't seem to notice them indicating that it is a one-way mirror. *We are invisible to the suspect. This must be the observation room,* Suryakant thinks.

Suddenly, the door opens and Arif enters. He stands next to them and hands a mini water bottle to Vikram.

Why is this guy always so serious? Suryakant wonders.

Vikram then goes and opens the door of the sub-room in which the suspect is sitting. Suryakant looks at Arif but Arif keeps looking at the suspect like a hawk looking at its prey.

"Why am I being held like a criminal?" the suspect asks in an angry tone. "It's been more than an hour that I am sitting here. I am a reputed doctor and I have to attend to my patients. You can't just hold me like this!"

Vikram patiently listens to him and then hands over the water bottle. "My apologies for the inconvenience doctor! But we are just trying to do our job. We have to ask a few questions for the record here. This will not take much time, sir."

The suspect calms down upon hearing the apology and being addressed as *"sir"*. He picks up the mini bottle and drinks it in one gulp. Vikram takes a sigh of relief.

"So, what are the questions?"

Vikram looks at his watch. "Just a minute, sir. Let me put on the video recorder." In a very slow manner, he picks up the video recorder and places it on the table. He sets up the video recorder. Then, he again looks at his watch and after a while presses the record button.

The suspect suddenly goes to sleep.

Vikram says, "The time is 1:22 PM. The interrogation of Dr. Sumit Mehta starts."

What is your name?
Sumit Mehta

Do you know Suman Mehta?
Yes.

What is your relationship with Suman Mehta?
She is my wife.

How many wives do you have?
One.

When was the last time you saw her?
On the morning of 24th September before I left for the hospital.

Did you kill your wife?
No.

Did you have any role in the disappearance of your wife?
No.

Do you know where your wife is right now?
No.

Have you received any ransom call regarding your wife after her disappearance?
No.

Vikram closes the video recorder. He picks up the bottle and video recorder and leaves the room. He now takes out the paper from his pocket and strikes out the name of Dr. Sumit Mehta.

Vikram and Arif start to leave the room. Suryakant follows.

What just happened inside? Suryakant wonders in astonishment but doesn't have the gumption to say anything.

❖ ❖ ❖

IR-2, CIU

September 5, 1:30 PM

They all enter the IR-2. It's like *deja-vu*. Almost a replica of the scene in the earlier room except that it is now suspect number two who is seated on the chair.

Arif takes out another bottle from his bag and hands it over to Vikram. Suryakant continues to watch in bewilderment. Vikram enters the room of the suspect. "How are you, Mr. Roshan Verma?"

"I am fine. Who are you?"

"I am Vikram Rathod, Special Investigator handling the case of disappearance of Mrs. Suman Mehta. Do you have anything to do with it?"

Roshan is in no mood to cooperate. He is displeased for being called and made to sit like a suspect. He makes his displeasure known, "I am sitting here for more than an hour. You cannot question me without my lawyer. I want my lawyer."

"Yes, your lawyer is on the way. We will question you in front of him only. Please calm down. Here, have some water."

Vikram places the bottle on the table and starts to set-up the video recorder.

Five minutes have passed but the suspect has not gone for the bait. He neither moves nor has shown any hint of picking up the bottle. The tension on Vikram's face is rising. He wants to avoid the 'other' option and continues to play with the video recorder for some more time. Then suddenly Roshan picks up the bottle and drinks it. Both Arif and Vikram are relieved.

Vikram again looks at his watch. After a while, he turns the recorder on. Roshan goes into sleep. Vikram says, "The time is 1:38 PM. The interrogation of Mr. Roshan Verma starts."

```
What is your name?
Roshan Verma.

Do you know Suman Mehta?
Yes.

What is your relationship with Suman Mehta?
Suman is a friend.

Is your relationship with Suman Mehta sexual
in nature?
Yes.

When was the last time you saw her alive?
Around  1  PM  in  the  afternoon  of  24th
September.

Is Suman Mehta alive?
No.

Did you kill Suman Mehta?
Yes.

Who all helped you in the  murder  of  Suman
Mehta?
Badrinath.

Is Badrinath the home servant of Suman Mehta?
Yes.
```

Vikram looks at his watch and realizes it's already one minute. He doesn't have much time left.

Where is the body of Suman Mehta?
It is kept in the freezer in the basement of my house.

What is the address of the house?
House No. 11A, Sector 37, Rajiv Nagar Extension, Rohini.

Where is the entrance to the basement of your house?
Through the garage, there is a secret entrance right under the car parking.

What is the reason for murdering Suman Mehta?
I was having an extra-marital affair with Suman Mehta. She was asking me to divorce my wife, failing which she was threatening that she would tell everyone.

How did you kill Suman Mehta?
I put her in the freezer and then slit her throat with a knife.

Where is the knife that you used to slit the throat of Suman Mehta, kept?
It is in the freezer.

Why did Badrinath help you?
I gave rupees ten lakhs to him for his help.

How did Badrinath help you?
He added sleeping pills in Suman Mehta's breakfast and then helped me take her to my house in the car.

Where is the car of Suman Mehta which she drove on 24th September?
The car was driven and dumped in Dada Mandu

Lake in Karala village, Delhi.

Vikram looks at his watch and realizes it's almost time. He closes the video recorder, picks up the bottle and leaves the room in a haste.

Suryakant looks on in amazement. *Am I dreaming or did this really happen? Did he just confess to everything?*

Vikram reads Suryakant's pale face. He knows that Suryakant is thinking that this is all a "magic" trick. *You have only witnessed "the Pledge" and "The Turn". Wait for "The Prestige".* He nonchalantly, takes out the sheet and strikes off suspect number three and places tick marks on suspect number two and four.

Arif says to Vikram, "I will get the warrant to search his place and Badrinath. I will send another team to trace the car and murder weapon."

Vikram nods. "There is no need to interrogate suspect number three. We can directly move to suspect number four." He picks up the intercom in the room and dials a three-digit number. "Has the home servant Badrinath arrived?" After a brief pause, he says, "Very well, get him to IR-4 and wait for me."

Arif dials a number from his cell phone. "Mukesh, Get the paperwork ready for search warrant at the residence of Roshan Verma and Badrinath."

"Suryakant come with me." A numb and speechless Suryakant follows.

Roshan Verma wakes up from sleep and sits as if he had a dream, which he is not able to remember. They all leave the room and start moving towards IR-4.

IR-4, CIU
September 5, 1:58 PM

Vikram enters the room and keeps the bottle on the table. "Drink some water. It is going to be a while." Vikram starts setting up the video-recorder as Badrinath drinks the water.

As Badrinath goes to sleep, the interrogation starts.

What is your name?
Badrinath Sharma.

Do you know Suman Mehta?
Yes.

What is your relationship with Suman Mehta?
I am the servant at her home.

When was the last time you have seen Suman Mehta alive?
In the morning of 24th September around 10 AM.

Did you add sleeping pills in the breakfast you gave to Suman Mehta on 24th September?
Yes.

On whose instruction did you add the sleeping pills?
Roshan Verma.

Why did you help Roshan Verma with the murder of Suman Mehta?
I needed money for the treatment of my wife.

How much money did Roshan Verma pay you for helping him with the murder of Suman Mehta?
Ten Lakh rupees.

Where are the ten lakh rupees kept?
At the house of my brother-in-Law.

What is the address of your brother-in-law?
B-43, Block-F, Sector-11, Dilshad Garden.

Do you know where the body of Suman Mehta is?
No.

Did you know that Roshan Verma was going to murder Suman Mehta?
Yes.

Vikram comes out of the room with the video-recorder and the bottle. He hands over the bottle to Arif.

"So, it's *18-0,*" Arif says in a congratulatory tone.

Vikram shakes hands with Arif. "I will go and inform the boss. You start the process for sending our teams to gather the victim's body, murder weapon, car and the money."

SI-3, CIU

September 5, 5:30 PM

Suryakant sits in his room, replaying the day's events in his head, over and over again.

He finally finds a moment to look around his office. Everything is new in the room - table, chair, computer, TV, printer, a three-seater sofa and a single seater sofa with table. He opens the drawer in his table. A file is kept which is marked as PROFILE. It is marked as CONFIDENTIAL. He takes out the file and opens it. It has a one-page profile of all the members of CIU. *That is an effective way of knowing your team.*

The profile of all the members is quite unique. He notices the key aspects in the profile

Ajay Raj Singh, 55 years, Home State U.P., IPS batch of 1994, AGMUT cadre, B. Sc. in Mathematics from St. Stephens College, Special skills: Hostage Negotiation.

Vikram Rathod, 42 years, Home State Rajasthan, IPS batch of 2011, AGMUT cadre, B. Tech in Electronics Engineering from IIT Kanpur, Special Skills: Hacking.

Arif Khan, 40 years, Home State U.P., IPS batch of 2013, Maharashtra cadre, B. Com. from Shri Ram College of Commerce, Special Skills: Black belt in Taekwondo.

He notices that even his profile is kept in the folder.

Suryakant Singh, 29 years, Home State Delhi, IPS batch of 2023, AGMUT cadre, B. Tech in Chemical Engineering from IIT Bombay, M.S. (Chemistry) from the University of Chicago.

The special skills field is blank in Suryakant's profile. *Nephew of the boss*, he is embarrassed to think. His profile looks more like that of a professor or a researcher and not that of a police officer. But circumstances have brought him here today. He closes his eyes to take a dip into his past. *Come out of the past.* Suryakant sighs and opens his eyes. Before he can turn the page to read the profile of the staff posted with him, there is a knock and the door opens.

Vikram enters the room. Suryakant keeps the folder down and immediately stands up to attention. "Sir."

"You are very lucky to witness the way we solve a case on your very first day. The victim's body, murder weapon and car have been recovered."

It had hardly been three hours. The teams went in with clear instructions about what to look for and where to look. "That was fast, sir."

"Yes, that's what we are here for. However, there is a problem. The money is still being traced. It seems the brother-in-law of the servant has fled with it. The police are trying to locate him. As of now, we have arrested Roshan Verma. He admitted to the crime after the body was recovered from his home. Your suspicion about the home servant was right. He is being held for questioning. We cannot arrest him as of now. Roshan in his confession statement in front of his lawyer has stated that he was acting alone and has no accomplice. So, for now, the home servant gets away."

Suryakant feels sad hearing this. *Why would he not mention the servant in his confession? Maybe the lawyer advised him not to do so.* His expression changes, which Vikram notices.

"What we know cannot be told or used anywhere. If we can trace the money, maybe we can get him later. For now, we have to live with this ugly truth."

Suryakant listens to what Vikram said. He understands the fine line on which CIU is treading.

"Do you have any questions?" Vikram asks knowing how Suryakant must be feeling. He still remembers the day he conducted his first interrogation with the weapon.

"Is what we are doing legal?"

"No. We are administering the suspects and questioning them without their consent. But the good part is that even the suspects don't have any recollection of their interrogation. So, the whole thing remains a secret. You are only the fourth person to know about this in CIU. Even the Home Minister does not exactly know what we do."

"What is in the bottle?"

"Water," Vikram replies as he smiles.

"And, what is in the water?"

"It is our astra (weapon) against crime. The less anyone knows about it, the better."

"What do we do if someone refuses to drink the water?"

"Normally, we make the suspect sit for a few hours ensuring that the suspect is feeling thirsty. In case the suspect still doesn't drink, then, as a last resort we inject them. But that is the last resort."

"How frequently can it be used?"

"We have a standing instruction that the weapon can only be used once on a suspect. We only get one chance to question any suspect and crack the case. So, the timing has to be right, not too early, nor too late. Normally, we get a case after the police has done the initial investigation, so we already have most of the information that we need."

"How much time does it take for it to take effect and how much time do we get to question the suspects?"

"It takes about 20 seconds once they drink the water. We get around 3 minutes to question them. After that, the effect of the weapon starts to wear out. We should be out of the room, by then. The person, once awake has no recollection of even drinking any water from the bottle. They may not even recall you coming in."

"And whatever they say during interrogation is the

truth?"

"Yes. We haven't seen anyone beat it so far."

"What do we call it?"

"TS-108"

"From where did we get it?"

"I don't know. Only the boss knows. And I never tried to find out. Boss is very clear about it."

Suryakant thinks that TS must mean "Truth Serum". *What does 108 mean?*

He knows 108 is a very special number in Science, Mathematics as well as in Indian religions.

In Science, the distance of Earth from the Sun is about 108 times the diameter of the Sun. The distance between the Earth and the Moon is about 108 times the moon's diameter.

Mathematically, 108 can be represented as $1^1.2^2.3^3$. 108 is a *Harshad* number, which is an integer divisible by the sum of its digits (*Harshad* is from Sanskrit and means "great joy"). 108 is also called an abundant number. In number theory, an abundant number or excessive number is a number for which the sum of its proper divisors is greater than the number itself. The integer 12 is the first abundant number.

Spiritually, there are said to be 108 earthly desires in mortals. There are said to be 108 lies that humans tell. There are supposed to be 108 human delusions or forms of ignorance. The chakras are the intersections of energy lines, and there are said to be a total of 108 energy lines converging to form the Heart Chakra.

In Hindu religion, the malas used while praying have 108 beads. The digits of 108 add to number 9 which is also very important. Keeping the importance of number 9, Rishi Vyasa has created 9 Puranas, 108 Mahapuranas (Upanishads). Mahābhārata has 18 chapters, Gita has 18 chapters, Bhagavat has 108000 *Shlokas* (verses). There are 54 letters in the Sanskrit alphabet. Each has masculine and feminine, *shiva* and *shakti*, 54 times 2 is 108.

In Buddhism, 108 is reached by multiplying the senses, smell, touch, taste, hearing, sight, and consciousness by whether they are painful, pleasant or neutral, and then again by whether these are internally generated or externally occurring, and yet again by past, present and future, finally we get 108 feelings. $6 \times 3 \times 2 \times 3 = 108$.

In Jainism, the total number of ways of Karma influx is governed by 4 *kashays* (anger, pride, conceit, greed) x 3 karanas (mind, speech, bodily action) x 3 stages of planning (planning, procurement, commencement) x 3 ways of execution (own action, getting it done, supporting or approval of action).

Suryakant gets lost in the significance of number 108. *Maybe that is why the Truth Serum has been named TS-108. It controls everything in the individual. The name is intelligently kept.*

Sensing there are no more questions, Vikram says, "You are part of this now, whether you agree with the method or not."

Suryakant promptly replies, "Sir, I want to be a part of this. Crime has increased a lot. Crime and criminals destroy our society. Rules have to be bent to restore the balance. Sometimes the end justifies the means."

"There are some internal rules that have to be followed to prevent any misuse of this weapon. First, the suspect needs to be asked specific questions of fact, not opinions or views. For instance, you can't ask the suspect whether you wanted to kill the victim.

Second, we can use it only for a case under investigation. We can't use it to ask anything random, even if it involves any other potential crime.

Third, the usage of TS-108 has to be done through proper procedure. It needs to be approved by the boss. He is the one who keeps an absolute control. One of us has to be present at the time of interrogation by the other.

So, respect the rules."

Suryakant nods and says, "I understand, sir."

"We may be crucified if the public or media comes to know about our secret weapon. So, whatever happens within the four walls of this office, should remain here. We are all taking a big risk."

"Whatever it takes, sir!" Suryakant nods.

Finally, Vikram moves his right hand forward and says, "Welcome to CIU." Suryakant shakes his hand and smiles back.

This weapon is the beginning of the end of crime, Suryakant marvels.

Vikram types a text to the Chief.

"He is in."

PART II

PARAM RAHASYA
(THE ULTIMATE MYSTERY)

कर्मण्येवाधिकारस्ते मा फलेषु कदाचन ।
मा कर्मफलहेतुर्भूर्मा ते संगोऽस्त्वकर्मणि ।।

कर्तव्य कर्म करने में ही तेरा अधिकार है फलों में कभी नहीं।
अतः तू कर्मफल का हेतु भी मत बन
और तेरी अकर्मण्यता में भी आसक्ति न हो ।।

Do your duty, but do not concern yourself with the results.
We have the right to do our duty,
but the results are not dependent only upon our efforts.

[Bhagavad Gita, Chapter 2, Verse 47]

Chapter 10
Asambhava
(Unthinkable)

Residence, Karol Bagh
November 8, 11:13 PM

His heart pounds abnormally fast. The shirt and trousers that he is wearing are covered in blood. With his shaky, blood-soaked hands, he wipes the tears from his eyes, but they continue to pour. Fighting his de-capacitated state, he gathers all the energy to take out his phone. Not able to decide whom to call, he dials '100'.

The phone rings twice and then a lady responds.

"Namaskar. Please state your emergency."

Sobbing between words, he says, "Shr…Shruti…She is…she is covered in blood…She…lying on the floor…not responding."

The voice from the other side wavers and asks, "Please provide your name and address."

"My name is…my name is Sudarshan and I am calling from my home…Bungalow No. 43, Street No. 8, Sector-13, Karol Bagh," he manages to tell the details in a shaky voice.

The lady types the address on her computer and marks it "URGENT".

"Please check if the victim is breathing or not. Check the pulse and inform."

"She is not breathing…and…I can't feel…I can't… find the pulse." The crying gets louder.

"Sir, please wait. Medical assistance will be sent immediately. Meanwhile try giving CPR if you know the procedure."

"I have already tried that. Please send someone… soon…" The other side hangs up the phone.

She immediately rushes to the command room where all calls that come to Delhi Police Control Room (PCR) are recorded. She tells the supervisor to play the last call received on line 4 immediately. The call is played back, and she is relieved that she has got the address correctly. She then calls and intimates the urgent situation to the officer-in-charge.

The officer in-charge calls the dispatcher's command room to ensure that they understand that this is a high priority situation, and that a PCR van and an ambulance needs to get there quickly.

❖❖❖

Residence, Karol Bagh
November 8, 11:29 PM

An ambulance arrives at the bungalow. Sudarshan hears a loud siren sound outside the home. He opens the door. A doctor and a nurse come out of the ambulance and rush inside.

"Where is the victim? Please take us to her immediately."

Sudarshan guides them.

PCR van arrives two minutes later. Police Inspector Balkrishna Chaube, a typical overweight inspector, alights along with two police constables.

As they move towards the bathroom, they see footsteps of blood made by Sudarshan. The doctor enters the bathroom and is startled by the scene he witnesses. A lady is lying on the floor covered in blood. The blood has already coagulated suggesting that it's been a while since the victim has died. With very low hope, he checks the pulse. He feels nothing.

He gets up and says, "She is dead. There is nothing we can do."

Sudarshan is sitting on the floor with his head cupped in his hands and his crying continues.

The doctor goes and whispers in the ear of Inspector Chaube, "This seems to be a crime scene. Seal the room and inform your seniors."

Inspector Chaube immediately instructs the two police constables to go and seal the room. He rushes to the PCR van and picks up the handset on the radio.

"This is Inspector Balkrishna Chaube reporting from Bungalow No. 43, Street No. 8, Sector-13, Karol Bagh. There is a dead body. The victim is a lady of around 50 years. She was found dead when the doctors arrived. The case appears to be high-profile. Probably a murder. Send an

Investigation team. Over."

"Noted. An investigation team is being sent. Please wait for further instructions. Over," replies the voice, on the other side of radio.

Residence, Karol Bagh
November 8, 00:15 AM

A police van reaches the spot. The door next to the driver's seat opens and a young man in his mid-thirties steps out of the van. He is wearing a black shirt and blue jeans and has a small beard. Following him, a photographer and a forensics team of two also step out from the back seat. The neighbors have gathered outside the house due to the arrival of police vehicles.

Inspector Chaube realizes that it is ACP Ashutosh Arora. He comes running and greets the senior officer.

"Sir," he says as they both move towards the house. "The victim is Shruti Chatterjee, 52 years old. We found her dead in the bathroom when we arrived. The husband Sudarshan Chatterjee had called on number 100 for help. He is the only one present and is also covered in blood. I have sealed the crime scene."

Ashutosh's eyes are quickly scanning the place. He knows exactly what to look for. "Is there any sign of a break-in?"

"No, sir. We did not notice anything broken nor is there any sign of forceful entry or escape."

"Anything stolen?"

"No, sir." He answers even though he has not checked for it.

"Are there any CCTV cameras in the house or in the neighborhood?"

"No, sir. No CCTV is installed."

"What is the cause of death?"

"The doctor said it appears that the death happened due to heavy loss of blood owing to multiple wounds on the head. The doctor also said she appears to have died at least an hour before they arrived." With a brief pause and to impress the senior, he says, "Sir, it is an open and shut case. It is clear that husband has killed the wife. We should arrest him immediately."

ACP and the Inspector reach the bathroom. Ashutosh carefully looks at the body and the scene. There is blood all around. The face is completely covered in blood. He has never seen so much blood before. It looks as if she tried to move but slipped over the blood again and again. Footprints of a person are seen on the blood on the floor beside the victim. *It must be of the husband*, ACP thinks to himself.

He walks out of the bathroom and stands in the bedroom as the photographer is clicking the photographs. The forensics team has also started to look for fingerprints and collect evidence.

"You said the husband made the call to number 100 asking for help. Why will you murder your wife and then call the police for help?" ACP asks.

"Must have murdered her in the heat of the moment. And then trying to look innocent he called the police himself to make it appear like an accident. He is educated, so must be a smart guy. This is a deliberate ploy to confuse the police. But he doesn't know that we solve such cases very frequently sir..." the inspector answers.

ACP is not impressed and asks, "How many members are there in the family?"

Inspector Chaube picks up a family photograph from the side-table to the bed and says, "Sir, apart from husband and wife, they have a daughter and son. The daughter is working somewhere in Noida and son is in college. The neighbors have told us."

"Was anyone at home when the incident happened?"

"No, sir."

"Where is the husband?"

"He is held in the other room. Please come, sir."

They both enter the other room. Sudarshan is sitting on the floor with both his hands on the face.

"Sir, I am ACP Ashutosh Arora, Investigating Officer for this case. I would like you to change your clothes. We will need them and some of your other belongings for the purpose of evidence," ACP tells Sudarshan.

"Evidence purpose! You think I killed my wife, officer?" Sudarshan says in an agitated but helpless voice.

"No, sir. We are just trying to do our job. Right now everything is potential evidence and we need to avoid any possible contamination. If you have not done anything wrong, you have nothing to fear. I understand what you must be going through, but right now we need your cooperation to get to the bottom of this," ACP says in a calm tone.

His words calm Sudarshan down. He changes his clothes and the same are put in a polythene bag. The slippers and cell phone phone are also handed over to the forensics team. ACP Ashutosh Arora asks Sudarshan to sit down.

"Please tell me in detail what happened tonight."

Residence, Karol Bagh
November 9, 00:45 AM

Sudarshan starts recollecting the dreadful events of the night...

We both were drinking wine and were relaxing on the terrace after dinner. I think the doorbell rang or some sound came, I'm not sure and Shruti went downstairs to check. I kind of dozed off that time.

After a while I woke up. She had not come back. I knew she wouldn't leave me dozing off alone on the terrace for so long. It was then I started to call for her.

"Shruti... Shruti..."

There was no response. I got up and started walking anxiously towards the stairs.

I called for her again, "Shruti... Where are you?"

I climbed down the stairs and switched on the light. There was no response whatsoever. I went to the drawing room but found the front door to be closed, so I knew she had not gone out.

I went to the bedroom. I did not see her. But then I heard some sound from the bathroom. The bathroom door was slightly open. I pushed the door to open it.

To my horror I noticed Shruti lying on the floor unconscious completely covered in blood. I picked her head up, kept it on my lap and tried to awaken her. But there was no response. She did not appear to be breathing and there was no pulse. It was then I decided to call the police.

Sudarshan returns to reality and starts to sob again.

He has narrated the events without asking for a lawyer. ACP realizes the person is in shock.

"Who do you think was at the door?" ACP asks.

"I don't know."

"Were you expecting anyone?"

"Nobody I can think of."

"What do you think happened to your wife?"

"I don't know."

"She must have shouted for help. You did not hear anything?"

"No. I did not hear anything."

"Can you think of anyone who might try to kill your wife?"

"I can't think of anyone."

"You said the front door was closed when you came down. Whoever had come must have left."

"I think so."

"Does anyone else stay in the house like a driver, or a house servant?"

"Yes, our house servant Radhey stays with us. But his brother was not well, so he left for his village near Sonepat this morning to see him."

Either he is too smart or too dumb. A very convenient story, with so many loopholes. Maybe Inspector Chaube was right, this is a simple case of murder of wife by husband, ACP Ashutosh Arora says to himself.

Ashutosh asks Inspector Chaube to keep an eye on Sudarshan and leaves the room. He goes to the terrace to verify the story he just heard. It's dark and there are no lights, so he takes out his cell phone, turns on the torch in it and carefully starts to walk. There are four chairs around a coffee table. Two glasses, two bottles and an ice-cube container are lying on the table. The glasses are empty and so are the bottles. He picks up one of them, smells it and then calls for the forensics team to take them as evidence. The forensics team is instructed to collect all possible evidence and seize all the computers, diaries, pen drives, etc., anything which may seem relevant.

He walks down and goes back to meet Sudarshan.

"Sir, right now you need to come with us to the police station for some paperwork."

Police Station, Karol Bagh
November 9, 10 AM

It is a cloudy day. There is a chill in the air signaling *Winter is coming.* Kritika, Ayushman, Deepak Agarwal, Indu Mehra and family friend Satish Kapoor reach the police station together. It's a two-storied building, freshly painted in light yellow color. Many police officials, reporters and cars are in the compound. There is a lot of activity outside the station, but the atmosphere is gloomy.

Deepak asks one of the constables sitting at the entrance, "Who is handling the case of Shruti Chatterjee?"

The uninterested, lazy looking constable responds, "ACP Ashutosh Arora. Room No. 9," and points them in the direction of room no. 9.

They all slowly move towards the room trying to look around and get a view of Sudarshan in any of the rooms. There is no trace of Sudarshan. They reach the desired room and read 'ACP Ashutosh Arora' on the door. Deepak knocks on the door.

The voice from inside calls, "Yes."

They all enter the room. Ashutosh is sitting at the table. Many files are kept on his table and he is looking at photographs in a file kept in front of him. Seeing them, he closes the file.

"Sir, I am Deepak Agarwal and she is Indu Mehra. We are Sudarshan's office colleagues. This is Kritika and Ayushman, daughter and son of Sudarshan Chatterjee. He is Satish Kapoor, a family friend. Can we get to meet Sudarshan?"

"Has he been arrested?" Satish intervenes.

Ashutosh gets up from his chair and moves closer to them. He looks at all of them trying to recall their names. He is not very good at remembering names. "He is in custody right now and we are questioning him. He hasn't been arrested yet. I need to take your statements before I allow you to meet him."

"Mr. Agarwal, madam and family friend, please wait outside. I have something to ask the daughter and son."

Realizing that they don't have much of an option, they do as instructed. As they leave the room Ashutosh moves closer to Ayushman and Kritika.

He sits on the table and asks them, "How was the relationship between your father and mother?"

"They were happily married. My father loved my mother more than anything in the world," Kritika replies instantly. Ayushman says, "They are the best parents one can hope for."

"What you are trying to imply is unthinkable,

impossible!" Kritika continues.

"You both stay away from parents; how much will you really know about their relationship?"

"I moved out just six months back. Before that I was living with them. I talked with both Mumma and Baba daily. I visited every weekend. I know how much they loved each other."

Ayushman joins in, "Baba is innocent."

They both start crying.

As Ashutosh tries to calm them down, a constable enters the room with Radhey. "Sir, this is Radhey - the house servant. We got him picked up from his brother's house."

Radhey moves forward, looking terrified. He has never been to a police station in his entire life. The police constable has picked him up from his brother's home. The constable has continuously threatened him on the way that in case he lies, *third degree* will be ensured. Radhey gets his hands together and prays, "Sir ji, I am innocent."

Ashutosh asks him, "Radhey, why did you go to your brother's house yesterday morning?"

"Sir, my brother was not well for quite some time. Yesterday, Sahabji told me to visit my brother and gave me two thousand rupees. I did not steal anything."

"And you were at your brother's place the entire day and night?"

"Yes, sir."

"How was the relationship between your Sahab and madam?"

"It was okay, sir."

"Did they have a fight in the last week or month over

something?"

"Nothing that I can remember of."

Ajay continues to look at Radhey without saying anything. A pause in a conversation can work wonders. It compels the other person to say something, even when there is no need to. Sensing that he needs to speak more, Radhey says, "But Sahab was in lot of tension for some time."

"Do you know what it was about?"

"I do not know for sure but maybe it was work related tension."

ACP Ashutosh presses a bell and tells the constable to send the office guys in and make these people sit out.

Deepak and Indu enter the room. Kritika, Ayushman and Radhey leave the room. Kritika and Ayushman still have tears all over their faces.

"So…you both were close to Mr. and Mrs. Sudarshan?"

"Yes, we were like family."

"How was their relationship?"

"They seemed to be doing okay. But I can't say for sure. Off late Sudarshan had a lot on his mind due to office troubles," Deepak replies. Indu doesn't say anything.

Ashutosh senses he is on to something. "Radhey also mentioned that there was some tension in the office. What was it?"

"Yes sir, the company is going through some financial troubles. Sudarshan had invested nearly all of their combined savings. Now he was planning to mortgage or sell his house as well. Shruti was not in favor of this. So, maybe this was the cause of tension."

"Who was the owner of the house?"

"The house was owned by Shruti," Deepak replies.

"Do you think he can murder his wife for it?"

"No, sir," Deepak answers. Indu just nods again.

People have killed for a lot less, Ashutosh thinks in his mind. "Please wait outside."

Kritika and Ayushman could hear the conversation from outside the room. As they come out of the room, Kritika glares at Deepak. *You liar...* The look hits Deepak hard. Kritika had no idea about the plans to mortgage their house and felt that by saying these things, Deepak had given police a motive.

Kritika looks at Satish and says, "Satish uncle, do you know any good criminal lawyer?"

Ayushman gets a call from Vaidehi and he steps aside to take the call.

Satish answers, "I know one. Let us go and meet him. They won't let us meet Sudarshan till we have a lawyer with us."

Inside the room ACP Ashutosh deliberates, *now we have a motive. I think the case is strong enough to arrest him. But we don't have any murder weapon. Let me wait for the post-mortem report!*

Chapter 11

PRATHAM
(THE FIRST CASE)

Chief's Cabin, CIU
November 9, 11 AM

It is a usual day at the office. Ajay Raj Singh is sitting on his chair sipping coffee and reading the newspaper. Politics and crime news interest him a lot. 'Police cracks another murder case', the news item gives him a lot of satisfaction. He takes pride in the fact that CIU has solved all the cases assigned to it so far. Whatever has been asked of him, he has delivered. There have been talks about him in the power corridors of North Block. His name is being considered for the top job at Delhi police, though he is the junior most in the race. He will be the youngest, if it happens. *The risk I took will pay off well!*

Suddenly, his cell phone rings. The call is from contact name 'Deepak Agarwal SSKA'. *Why is he calling?* He picks up the phone and answers the call.

"Hello."

"Good morning, sir. Sir, there is a big problem. The wife of Sudarshan Chatterjee, Shruti was found dead in the house last night. Sudarshan is in police custody. I just met the investigating officer ACP Ashutosh Arora at Karol Bagh police station. From what I could make out, it looks like they are going to charge him!"

Ajay looks at the television. *No murder news. The national media is yet to pick up the story.*

"What do you want from me?"

"Sir, I don't know who else to call. You need to do something. The police will look to close the case hastily until and unless you intervene. They don't want the truth but a quick closure."

Ajay weighs his words carefully while talking on the phone. Smartphones are with almost everyone these days, he has to be extra careful with what he says. "But I can't intervene in an ongoing police investigation."

Deepak is taken aback by the reply. "Sudarshan is a reputed person and certainly not a murderer. Also, this will be very bad for the company. We won't be able to survive this. Please help Sudarshan. You are our last hope."

"Let me see what I can do."

Ajay hangs up the phone and begins to weigh his options. Personal relationships should remain away from professional work. After five minutes of deliberation, he picks up his landline. "Please connect me to ACP Ashutosh Arora at Karol Bagh station." He receives a call back after ten minutes. The conversation lasts for nearly five minutes. As the call ends, he looks at the TV. *So, the story reaches the media.*

He picks up the phone and says, "Check if the Home Minister is in the office. If yes, fix up my meeting with the Home Minister within an hour. Say it's urgent."

Ajay anxiously waits for the confirmation of the meeting. In the meantime, he turns on the volume of the TV and listens to the news report.

Last night, Shruti Chatterjee, a 52 year old woman was found dead in her residence at Karol Bagh under very mysterious circumstances ...

The secretary calls back within five minutes. "Home Minister is in the office. They have given an appointment for 12:10 PM."

"Ask my driver to keep the car ready in ten minutes."

"Right, sir."

Home Minister's Office, November 9, 12:10 PM

Ajay enters the office and salutes the Home Minister. For a change, Mantriji's table does not have any files. Manohar has the habit of reading each and every note sheet put up to him, so it takes time for him to clear the files. He may be short in height but he is definitely not a pushover. His mind is as sharp as a razor and this has been the reason for his decisive command over the Ministry.

"Come Ajay. Please sit." Manohar pushes a box

towards him. "Have some of these."

Ajay picks up one piece and takes a bite. "Sir, why are these momos sweet?"

Manohar feels ridiculed by the remark. "These are not momos but modaks, a very popular sweet from Maharashtra. The Chief Minister is a dear friend of mine. He has sent it."

"My apologies, sir." *This is indeed awkward,* he feels.

Not impressed, Manohar directly switches to the purpose of the visit. "What was so urgent?"

"Sir, a crime story is developing on the death of the wife of Dr. Sudarshan Chatterjee. I have spoken to the investigating officer, ACP Ashutosh Arora. All the evidence so far suggests that it is a murder by the husband. But even he feels that the case is a bit odd. The case is already picked up by national media. I came to request you to hand this case over to CIU."

Surprised at the request, Manohar asks, "Is there something you are not telling me?"

Ajay does not answer immediately. He tries to figure out what Manohar has in his mind. Playing innocent, he finally says, "Not at all, sir."

Manohar notices the sudden tension on Ajay's face. Realizing he is not going to say anything further, Manohar says, "I have already received directions from the PMO that the case should be handed over to CIU. They want the case to be investigated on priority. Regular updates about the case must be given to PMO as well. So, I ask again, is there something you are not telling me?"

"Sir, I think the PMO has become interested because Dr. Sudarshan Chatterjee is a *Padma Shri* recipient. He received it a few years back. It is going to be a high-profile case and they probably expect a lot of media coverage on it."

Manohar narrows his eyes and gives a sharp look but Ajay is unmoved. Ajay had not expected this sudden turn of events but he remains composed. Unable to notice anything odd in his reaction, Manohar softens, "Alright. But any development in the case, I want to be updated first. Even before the information is given to PMO."

"Of course, sir."

"No screw-ups in the investigation. Keep a close watch on the case."

"Right, sir."

Manohar picks up the phone and directs his PA, "Connect me to the Commissioner of Police." After about two minutes, his phone beeps again. He picks it up and the PA says, "Sir, I have Commissioner of Police on line 2." Manohar presses line 2. "Gill, the case of the death of Shruti Chatterjee is to be handed over to CIU with immediate effect. This is to be done on priority."

Ajay thanks Mantriji and leaves the room.

Chief's Cabin, CIU

November 9, 1:15 PM

Ajay enters his room with a folder in his hand and tells the peon to call Suryakant.

After 2 minutes, Suryakant enters the room.

"Sir."

"Sit down." The voice is stern. "You have been part of CIU for nearly two months now. I think you are ready to investigate a case on your own." Pushing the file toward him, "The case has been assigned to CIU by the Home

Minister himself and it is being monitored by the PMO. The accused is a *Padma Shri* recipient, so you can understand the sensitivity of the case. I am assigning this case to you. Give your best and keep me updated about each and every development. This is the case file. Take charge."

Finally, I have my first case! But it looks like a very difficult one from Chief's tone. PMO is monitoring! "Sir, this is my first case. I will give it my best. You won't be disappointed." He camouflages his nervousness, takes the file and leaves the room.

SI-3, CIU
November 9, 1:30 PM

Many thoughts run through his mind as Suryakant goes back to his room and sits on the chair. He opens the file titled 'Case No. 27'.

The file has the report filed by ACP Ashutosh Arora. There are also some photographs of the crime scene from various angles. He has not seen so many actual photos of a victim before. The statement of the husband, Sudarshan Chatterjee, catches his attention. The narration in the statement is so vivid that Suryakant is effortlessly able to create a mental image of the events of that fateful night.

Husband and wife are on the terrace drinking. Husband is almost dozing off. There is a doorbell or some sound from downstairs. Wife goes downstairs leaving the husband. After about an hour husband wakes up and goes downstairs. He searches for his wife but gets no response. The main door of the house is locked. He hears something in the bathroom. He opens the door and finds his wife lying on the floor covered in blood. He immediately rushes to pick her up and tries to wake her. Sensing the worst, he calls '100'. The police arrives twenty minutes later. The doctor declares the wife dead for more than an hour. Police finds no evidence of break-in or presence of any other person. There is no CCTV footage available to verify the story. It is nighttime thus neighbors have not seen anything. There are no eyewitnesses.

Suryakant has a habit of writing things down. It helps him in organizing his thoughts. He starts jotting down his thoughts.

1. *Who is Shruti Chatterjee?*

2. *Murder or Accident?*

<u>Accident</u>

1. *Post Mortem report - not yet received*

2. *Husband called 100 for help*

<u>Murder by Husband</u>

1. *How was their relationship?*

2. *Against him*

    a. *They were alone at home - No other prints found near the body.*

    b. *Why exactly did the wife go downstairs?*

    c. *No evidence of anyone coming to the house.*

    d. *Did not hear the screams or voice of wife.*

    e. *Home servant sent away, the same morning.*

    f. *Nothing is found stolen or reported missing.*

    g. *Motive is there - mortgage of the house.*

3. *In his favor*

    a. *Children support him.*

    b. *He was drinking on the terrace.*

    c. *No eyewitness.*

4. *Could it be a heat of the moment accidental murder?*

a. Not confessing.

<u>*Murder by someone else?*</u>

1. Someone might have come.

2. Something might have been stolen.

As he feels a little headache developing thinking of the numerous possibilities, he presses the bell on the table.

The door opens and the peon says, "Yes, sir."

"Get me a coffee."

He recalls the investigation methodology followed by Vikram. Though normally CIU gets a case when regular police investigation has already been done and there is no result, this case has been handed over to CIU at a very preliminary investigation stage, so we can't immediately have the list of potential suspects. Even the post-mortem report and CDRs of victim and suspects are not available. It's too early to start writing down the names of suspects for putting them to test.

He takes out a blank paper from the printer paper tray.

1. Victim - Shruti Chatterjee

2. Husband - Sudarshan Chatterjee - owns company SSKA

3. Children - 1 daughter Kritika and 1 son Ayushman

4. SSKA - Deepak Agarwal, Indu Mehra, ...

5. Friends - Satish Kapoor, ...

6. Relatives - ??

He picks up the phone and tells inspector Brijesh to come to his room. Brijesh enters after a minute.

"Brijesh, this is regarding case no. 27. I need the CDRs for all the cell phone numbers belonging to the persons mentioned from 1 to 5. You should be able to access the scanned documents of the case from the server, get the details from there." He hands over the sheet to Brijesh.

"I also need the basic profile of all the persons prepared, with details such as date of birth, marriage, educational qualification, current job, past job, all known addresses, any earlier criminal record, etc."

"Yes, sir. Anything else, sir?"

"No. That's all for now. How much time will this CDR and profiling take?"

"Sir, CDR will take around 3 to 4 hours depending on the service providers. Profiling will take a couple of hours."

"Alright, get going."

As Brijesh is about to leave, Suryakant stops him. "Has the post-mortem report come?"

"I will find out, sir." Brijesh leaves.

Suryakant starts sipping the coffee on the table. Many thoughts are entering his mind. *For a murder you need - motive, murder weapon, witness, any forensic or circumstantial evidence or simply a confession.* But then a paradoxical thought comes to his mind - *If it's an accident, how will one know?*

He sighs. *I need to wait for the details. Also, I need to visit the crime scene once myself. Maybe there is something that the photographs or video missed!*

Chapter 12
Kalaṅka
(Disgrace)

Residence, Karol Bagh
November 9, 4 PM

A white police van stops outside the Bungalow. Suryakant steps out of the car and looks at the white-colored bungalow in front of him. He then takes a look around. There are two media cars parked outside, waiting for some activity. Inspector Pandey also steps out from the back seat. Two police constables are already standing outside the bungalow talking. They don't seem to have noticed the police van.

Noticing Suryakant, the reporters start moving towards the police van. Sensing some activity, the constables realize that some senior officer has come. Inspector Pandey stops the reporters and prevents them from approaching Suryakant.

"Is anyone at home?", Suryakant asks.

"Yes, sir. The daughter, son, two family friends and a servant are in the house. The crime room is locked." He takes out the key from his pocket and shows it.

No relatives have come till now! Are there none? Suryakant thinks to himself as he enters the house. Constable rushes ahead and opens the door.

Kritika is standing in the hall and talking on the phone. He could hear the words, "I want the best lawyer. Please Adi. Convince him to take the case." She hangs up the phone. They both make eye contact, but no words are spoken. Suryakant notices two boys and a man of around fifty years of age sitting on the sofa. *One of the boys must be Ayushman and maybe the middle-aged man is the family friend, Satish Kapoor.* They all get up. The aged man starts moving towards him.

Suryakant stays silent and avoids eye contact. He looks at the constable and says, "Which room?"

Constable quickly goes to the room and unlocks the bedroom. Suryakant takes out a pair of gloves and wears them. He carefully enters the room, making sure he does not touch anything. He takes a look at the room. There is a painting of Shiva-Parvati hanging on the wall, above the bed. He notices the name at the bottom 'Shruti'. It's a typical room with one double bed having side-tables, dressing table and two cupboards. There are around eight family photos on the wall. He identifies Kritika and Ayushman in the photos.

Suryakant walks towards the door in the room knowing that it must be the bathroom and pushes the door open. The room is dark as the sunlight does not have enough place to enter. He switches on the light and notices the blood stains and outline of the body, drawn on the floor. There are blood marks on the edge of the wash basin and on the toilet pot.

Did she accidentally hit her head here or is it because someone pushed her? He notices the blood marks of her left hand on the wall. *Did she try to get up?*

Coming out of the bedroom, he notices another family photo of four sitting on the side-table of the bed. As he crosses the verandah, he takes a look again at the several family photos on the wall. *A happy family*, he thinks.

For his satisfaction, he decides to inspect all the rooms one by one. He goes to the terrace as well. Finally, the room outside the bungalow, in the garden, encircling the big banyan tree catches his attention and he decides to go there. The room looks like a study cum meditation room. Many sculptures, paintings and pictures of Lord Shiva in various poses are placed around the room. There is even a photograph from Koneswaram Temple in Sri Lanka depicting Rāvaṇa sacrificing one of his heads to please Lord Shiva. It is quite rare to have a picture of Rāvaṇa displayed at one's home. The other depictions are of Shiva meditating, Shiva Tāndav, Nataraja and many more. Clearly, the person is a Shiva devotee. He goes around opening the drawers and looks at their content. There are many books and novels kept on a big bookshelf. The titles interest him. So, he picks out the books one by one and quickly turns the pages, looking for any note or writing on them. As he opens the fifth book and starts to turn the pages, a photo falls down. It is a photo of Sudarshan with a lady in their marriage clothes. *This is not Shruti.* He takes a deeper look, keeps the photo in his pocket and comes out of the room.

As he enters the drawing room again, Kritika and Ayushman who are still standing there are now joined by a servant. Another boy is sitting on the sofa quietly. Satish is out of the house taking a call.

Suryakant looks at Kritika. He couldn't ignore how graceful she looked in the white kurta and blue jeans. Her long, straight hair were not tied. He notices her dusky looks and big, round and penetrating eyes - quite distinctive to Bengali girls. Her teary eyes looked like she needed someone for comfort. It occurs to him that Shruti did not have such Bengali looks.

Suryakant goes towards Kritika and introduces himself, "I am Special Investigator Suryakant Singh. I will be investigating this case now."

He asks her, "How long were your parents married?"

"They were happily married for the last seventeen years." The stress is ostensibly on the word 'happily'.

Around seventeen years but she must be more than twenty years old. He asks, "Was this a second marriage for your father?"

She replies, "Yes," wondering how it was relevant.

"And you must be the daughter from an earlier marriage?"

She nods.

He looks at Ayushman, "Is he also from the first marriage or second marriage?"

Kritika replies, "No, he is my step-brother. He is from Mumma's first marriage." Suryakant could clearly feel the anger in her tone. She clearly did not like the line of questioning. But he notices the use of the word 'Mumma' for stepmother.

A complicated modern family, he thinks.

Kritika goes on talking, "We all were very happy together. There is no way Baba could have had any hand in the death of Mumma. It's a disgrace to even think of such a thing." She starts to cry.

Ayushman moves forward and finally speaks, "This is very hard for us. Mumma is gone but please at least send Baba back home. Whatever you may think, Baba is innocent. We know."

He senses that they sound very confident about Sudarshan having no role in the murder.

Suryakant looks at the other boy with him. "What is your name and who are you?"

He stands up and is very tense. He wasn't expecting any questions from the police. His voice shakes as he answers, "Sir, sir…my name is Prashant Mehra…I…I am Ayush's friend."

Kritika intervenes, "He is Indu aunty's son. They both are in the same college. He came to be with us for some moral support."

Feeling he has scared them, Suryakant asks Kritika, "Do you have any relatives?"

"Yes, my *bua* (aunt) lives in the US and *mamaji* (uncle) lives in Australia. They settled there many years ago."

"What do you both do? Do you stay in the house?"

"I am a reporter with 'News 360' news channel. For the last six months, I have taken a house in Noida as my office is there. But I come home every weekend. Ayushman is doing engineering here in Delhi. He stays in a hostel, but he keeps visiting every now and then."

Satish enters the house and starts listening to the conversation.

"Were your father and mother going through any mental tension, maybe related to business?"

"Baba never talked about work at home. Nevertheless, if he had such any tension, he would have definitely told us."

"Do you know your father was going through financial difficulties and was thinking of selling or mortgaging the house?"

Kritika stands quietly, still measuring the relevance of the question. *Baba never said anything about selling the house or financial difficulties. There were usual business problems.*

"Who told you this?" Kritika retorts in an angrier tone.

Suryakant does not answer.

Ayushman gets a call from Vaidehi but he doesn't take the call.

Satish steps into the conversation. "Sir, I am Satish Kapoor. I am a family friend. When will Sudarshan be released?"

Suryakant again doesn't answer, instead he asks Kritika, "If you don't mind, can you tell me what happened to your biological mother?"

"She died in an accident in 2004. I was two when she died."

"I am sorry to hear that. What was her name?"

"Veena Chatterjee."

Turning to Ayushman, Suryakant asks, "And what was the name of your biological father?"

"Rudra Trivedi," Ayushman answers.

Before he could question them further, Suryakant gets a call on his cell phone. *Boss is calling*

"Please call me in case you have any new information related to the case. Thank you for your time." Suryakant hands over his visting card and leaves abruptly.

SI-3, CIU
November 9, 6:30 PM

Suryakant walks into his office and sits on the chair. *Neither of the children seem to suspect their father. Even the son... Knowing that he is his stepfather. Strange!* Suryakant wonders

He realizes that a file is kept with 'Post-Mortem Report - Case No. 27' written on it. He opens the file and starts to read the key points.

<u>Observations:</u>

All clothes were intact, having no cuts or tears. Clothes were soaked with blood, particularly on the front aspect. There were minor cuts on the forearms, indicating possibility of struggle.

There were two visible fractures on the head, one severe and other minor. The severe fracture on the left side of the head was due to a cut of length 3 cm and breadth of 0.4cm made by a sharp-edged object. This cut resulted in severe internal and external bleeding. Bleeding from left ear and nose was also recorded. The loss of blood due to bleeding was also severe.

No other external injuries were present on the body.

There was presence of alcohol in the blood.

<u>Opinion - Cause of death:</u>

After overall considerations, cause of death is opined as "shock and hemorrhage as a result of multiple

head injuries."

He reads the name at the end of the report 'Dr. Ramakant Joshi', the in-house medical examiner. He picks up the intercom and calls him.

"Hello, please connect me to Dr. Joshi."

After some time, he hears, "Hello, this is Dr. Joshi."

"Doctor, I am Suryakant Singh. I was reading the post-mortem report of Mrs. Chatterjee. Do you think it was a murder or an accident?"

"Very difficult to say. It is like fifty-fifty."

"Ok. Thank you, doctor." *This is not very helpful!*

He hangs up the intercom.

Suryakant pushes back on the chair, puts both hands on top of his head and takes a deep breath. *An inconclusive post-mortem report. What should be my next step?*

He decides to hear the recording of the call made by Sudarshan to the emergency helpline number 100. He takes out the keyboard and mouse on his table which he has rarely used since he has joined. He clicks a few buttons on the mouse and types a few keys on the keyboard. Finally, he reaches the recording file. He puts on the headphones, plays the recording and starts to listen. He can sense the desperation and helplessness in Sudarshan' voice. He plays it again to see if he can get something more. He notices that in the call Sudarshan mentions that he has already given CPR to Shruti. However, during his statement, there is no mention of any CPR tried on Shruti by Sudarshan. *You tend to miss out when you are hiding something. Is he hiding something?*

Feeling a slight stiffness in his body, he gets up and does some stretches. He decides to take a fresh look at the case but before he can begin an image of Kritika suddenly appears in his mind. *She is indeed beautiful,* he thinks to himself. *Poor girl lost both of her mothers in such an unfortunate manner. What was the name of her biological mother?* he tries to recollect. *Veena Chatterjee.*

He clicks on the browser icon and goes to 'google. com'. Then he types "Veena Chatterjee 2004 accident" and presses enter button.

With patience, he looks at all the links one by one, but does not find anything relevant on the first page. With very little hope, he presses the button for the next page. The third link on the page draws his attention. He clicks on it and begins to read. It is a news report from October 11, 2004.

A 24-year old lady was found dead at her residence in Rajouri in New Delhi on Tuesday, a police official said. There was no one at home at the time of death. The husband who was at work, reported the incident to the police after he arrived home.

Inspector Nandkishore Sharma of the Rajouri police station told the media that the body of Mrs. Veena Chatterjee was found in the afternoon after her husband received a call from the crèche, informing him that their two-year old daughter had not been picked up by the mother.

"We have registered the case and further investigation is on," he added. The exact cause of her death would be known after the post-mortem.

However, the police officials suspect that it may be a case of freak accident. Maybe she slipped on the floor and died due to her head hitting the bathroom sink, a police official on condition of anonymity stated. However, the police have not ruled out murder and are exploring all possibilities.

Sensing he has found something, Suryakant presses the print button. The color printer slowly prints the page. He then picks up the page, bends backwards on his chair, and starts to read again. *Bloody hell. This can't be a coincidence. It's not a simple case of accident but is a case of double murder.*

A bout of rage fills him up. *How is it possible that the daughter does not see the resemblance? Maybe she doesn't even know yet!*

I need to meet this man. He can't get away. This is a dangerous and clever guy I am dealing with. It will be a disgrace to the police department and humanity if such a man gets away. I won't let that happen. I need the case file on Veena Chatterjee.

Suryakant gets up and leaves the room. His hatred for criminals - the reason he joined IPS, is evident on his face.

Chapter 13
Tat Mā Vada
(Don't say that)

IR-1, CIU
November 9, 8:30 PM

Suryakant enters the room and watches Sudarshan through the one-way mirror. He is wearing a white kurta-pajama. There is a *teeka* on his forehead, *rudraksha mala* in his neck and a red thread on his wrist.

After thinking for five minutes on how to play this, he decides to go in. *You can't hide behind this mask.* He enters the room with a smile.

"Good evening. How are you feeling?"

"How should a broken man feel?"

Broken. You are the one breaking everyone's trust! "How do you live with yourself?"

Sudarshan gets confused with the question but then he realizes that this is an interrogation for the death of his wife. They are treating him as a suspect. He feels it is best to not answer such questions.

"How do you get your daughter and son to trust you so much?"

Sudarshan keeps quiet realizing that it does not matter what he says.

"You know what. You can fool them but not me. I can see the real you."

"You are filled with confusion and rage. They blur your mind. You can't see anything with this."

He is smart enough to act dumb when needed. Suryakant gets even more angry. "Why don't you just confess, that will save everyone so much time. You were alone in the house with your wife, no one came to the door, her blood was all over your body, no other fingerprints were found - this is hard evidence. Post-mortem report says the death was due to heavy loss of blood. There were two wounds on her head which suggests she was hit. One can't get hit two times if it was an accident. If I were to talk of the motive - you wanted the house to save your company and she refused to give it up for the sake of your failing company…"

"Don't say that! I could never even in my dreams think of hurting my wife. I truly loved her."

"You know what, I don't trust you and neither will your family after they get to know about the real you."

"What do you mean - the *real* me?"

"Does your daughter and son know how your first wife died?"

There is a sudden change in Sudarshan's expression, as if the sky has fallen on his head. "How did you…" he stops. It is almost as if his breath has been snatched away.

"All your dirty secrets are going to come out. There is no way you are going to get away with this. The media will have a field day after hearing this story. Your daughter and son will hate you. Your friends and colleagues will despise you."

Sudarshan closes his eyes and a tear comes out of his left eye.

Suryakant continues, "Your reputation will be destroyed. The *Padma Shri* you received will be taken away."

"Please stop. I confess. Please just don't involve my family in all this."

Got it. He broke. "I will need your signed statement. You will have to confirm it before a magistrate as well." Suryakant is delighted that he has cracked his first case with a confession. And he didn't even need to break any law. *Beginner's luck?*

"I will. Just ensure that the memory of my first wife is not destroyed. My daughter and son don't know much about how she died. They think it was an accident. Please let it stay that way. I beg you. I will do whatever you say."

"You have my word, if you stick to yours." Suryakant gets up and leaves. Hurtful words are such that they pierce the heart and weigh down the soul. For the first time in his life, he feels proud of uttering them.

For the first time, they have served a noble purpose.

Chief's Cabin, CIU
November 9, 9 PM

Suryakant knocks and enters the room. He is visibly excited. "Sir, I have good news. The husband confessed. I got him to confess."

Ajay got elated and surprised at the same time, "How?"

"Sir, I dug more. I discovered the secret of how his first wife died. You won't believe it but she died under similar circumstances - almost the same style. When I confronted him, he confessed."

Ajay couldn't believe what he had just heard. His heart almost skipped a beat. "You found some evidence which connected the two deaths?"

"No Sir, I just questioned him. I told him the media will love this story if it is leaked to them. His son and daughter will hate him when this comes out."

"Did you read the case file of the first wife's death?"

"No, sir. I read a newspaper article." Pushing forward the newspaper printout.

Ajay takes the printout and reads it. After a while, he puts the paper down and shakes his head. "Suryakant, this is not the way we work here."

"Sir, I got him to confess and the case is solved!"

The boss doesn't appreciate the response. Mistakes, not corrected at the right time, become potential blunders for the future. A lesson needs to be taught. "What you did is pure blackmail! We are not here to just solve a case; we are here to uncover the truth by getting irrefutable evidence. We seek right answers, not any answer."

"But this is the truth, sir."

"You don't know the truth. You didn't even put in the effort to the read the case file before coming to me. I was the Investigating Officer for that case. From what I remember, it was an accidental death with absolutely no evidence of any foul play. He was not even near the house when it happened. That's how I know him. He is a very different guy. Spend some time with him and you will know. We are here to know the truth, not to get a coerced version of the truth. You forgot *Nānṛtaṃ* in our motto so soon. I expected more from you."

"But sir, he confessed now. Maybe something was missed in the earlier investigation."

"He may confess right now but will retract the confession later when the trial commences. What will you do then? I want you to get the truth, don't take the easy way out by forcing a confession. It's the habit of mediocre police officers to get confessions using coercion. Such cases do not stand a chance before the judiciary. This is the reason so many get away. Remember that."

With a small pause, he adds, "Either you grow or you go home."

Suddenly, all the enthusiasm of Suryakant disappears as if Thanos has snapped his fingers. The word 'mediocre' hits him hard. But he realizes what the boss is saying, is indeed right.

"And remember you are investigating the case of Shruti Chatterjee's death and not the case of death of his first wife. Go and read the case file first and find something that we 'missed'. The case is closed as of now. Until and unless you find something which makes me 'believe' and not 'suspect' that the death of the first wife could be a murder, you can't question the suspect on first wife's murder. So, no questioning on this, till the file is opened again. Is that understood?"

Suryakant is not able to comprehend why this condition has been imposed but he is in no position to question his boss right now. "Right sir."

A dejected Suryakant gets up and leaves the room with the voice in his head crying, *"Shame, Shame, Shame, …."*

As Suryakant leaves and the door closes, Ajay picks up his cell phone and makes a call.

SI-3, CIU
November 9, 9:30 PM

Suryakant returns to his room and sits on the chair. He feels as if he has been made to go through a "walk of shame" as in Game of Thrones and publicly humiliated. The word 'mediocre' is still ringing in his head. He tries to rationally think again. *I know it's him. He is a dangerous guy. I need the case file for the death of Veena Chatterjee.*

He picks up his phone and calls Brijesh. "Brijesh, have the CDR for all the numbers come?"

"Yes, sir. I am analyzing the CDRs received. I will get the analysis report in ten minutes."

"Get it done quickly. I also need the case file for the death of one Veena Chatterjee. She is first wife of Sudarshan Chatterjee. She died on October 11 in 2004 and the case was registered at Rajouri Police Station."

It occurs to Brijesh that boss wants a twenty-year-old case file. There are better chances of finding aliens than finding an old government record. "Sir, only the files after 2015 have been digitized. Anything prior to that has to be searched for manually. There is only a half chance that we will get it now," Brijesh replies.

Suryakant is in no mood to hear excuses. He trusts his instincts. "Yes, I want to take that half chance. Go and trace it yourself immediately. It's important for the case."

Brijesh turns to the wall clock. It is late in the day. But sensing the boss's mood and tone, he has no option but to comply, "Right, sir. I will go after giving you the CDR analysis report." Brijesh knows in his head that new recruits are always this way, detached from reality.

Suryakant tells him to put the CDR analysis report on his table and update him on the Veena Chatterjee case file in the morning. It is time to call it a day and start afresh early tomorrow.

SI-3, CIU
November 10, 8:30 AM

Suryakant enters the office early and finds the CDR report on his table. *No call from Brijesh till now, looks like he did not find it.* He calls Brijesh on his cell phone. "Any update on the case file?"

"Sir, I looked for it the entire night. It seems the file is missing."

Missing…that's surprising. "How is that possible?"

"Sir, it is possible that it might have been weeded out. The staff there is not sure. It's nearly twenty years old matter and the case was closed."

Possible but still surprising, he thinks. "Anyways, ask them to keep looking."

"Yes, sir, I have told them to keep looking."

This also turns out to be a dead end. But it is too much of a coincidence to ignore, he says to himself. He has to start somewhere else now. Suryakant takes a look at the CDR analysis report.

For obvious reasons, he first takes out Kritika's call record. She has maximum duration calls with Shruti, then Sudarshan, then Aditya Bajaj. The name catches his attention. He has heard this name before when he had gone to the house. *Who is this Aditya Bajaj? Her boyfriend, boss, friend?*

He moves to his keyboard and googles "Aditya Bajaj News 360". The first link he gets is the LinkedIn profile of Aditya Bajaj. He opens the link. The profile says Content Manager at "News 360" channel. His age is mentioned as 42 years. It's highly unlikely that he is her boyfriend. *Definitely boss!* There is a sense of relief.

He takes out his cell phone and saves Kritika's number. Her number appears on WhatsApp along with her profile pic. Suryakant keeps looking at the pic for nearly ten seconds. Something inside him is making him to do this. He does not understand, what.

Next, he takes out Shruti's call record analysis. Shruti has maximum duration of calls with Kritika, then Radhey, then with Sudarshan, then Ayushman, then Deepak Agarwal, then some doctor, rest are very insignificant. He then takes a look at calls on the day of her death. The last call before her death was with Kritika at 7:09 PM. The call pattern is quite as expected. *But why does she have so many calls with Deepak Agarwal? She has no position in the company.*

He takes out call record for Sudarshan. Maximum duration calls are with Kritika, then Shruti, then Indu, then his secretary, then Radhey, Ayushman, then Deepak, then….

The CDR analysis for other numbers does not show anything unusual.

There is nothing more to investigate. *It's time.* He decides to use the secret weapon TS-108. He calls Ajay sir on intercom and says, "Sir, I want to use TS-108 on Sudarshan. Need your authorization."

"You have my authorization. I will meet you in IR-1 in ten minutes."

With such a quick approval, Suryakant senses that Ajay was waiting for his request call. He himself wants to be present during interrogation tells him that he is quite interested in the case. *Is it because of the pressure from higher ups?,* he wonders.

He soon gathers himself. *This will be my first interrogation with TS-108 in IR-1.*

IR-1, CIU
November 10, 9 AM

Sudarshan is sitting in the interrogation room. Suryakant stands outside looking at him and is in deep thought. *This is my guy. I need to get evidence to establish that he is the murderer. What evidence do I need - the murder weapon, motive…? Should I ask him about his first wife? But Ajay sir will be watching and he has been very clear about the internal rules that no questions beyond the present case can be asked...*

He is still working out the line of questioning in his mind, when Ajay Raj Singh enters the room.

He asks Suryakant, "Are you ready?"

"Yes, sir."

"Remember the rules - No questions beyond the

current case."

Suryakant nods, "Yes, sir."

Ajay hands over a bottle to him and says, "I will be watching. All the best."

Suryakant takes the bottle and enters the room. "Good morning, officer. When do I write my confession?", Sudarshan asks inquisitively.

"Good morning. We will do that in a while. But before that please have some water."

Sudarshan takes the bottle and gulps it in one go. Suryakant sets up the video camera and looks at the time.

After about thirty seconds, Sudarshan goes to sleep. Suryakant says to himself, *Here we go!*

"The interrogation of Sudarshan Chatterjee starts at 9:08 AM at IR-1."

> What is your name?
> *Sudarshan Chatterjee.*
>
> What is the name of your wife or wives?
> *Shruti Trivedi and Veena Chatterjee.*

Ajay Raj Singh narrows his eyes. He says to himself, *Be careful Suryakant. Don't go there.*

> When is the last time you had seen Shruti Chatterjee?
> *On the night of 11th October around 11:45 PM.*
>
> Did you kill Shruti Chatterjee?
> *No.*

Don't say that. Suryakant says to himself, *What should I ask now!* He realizes he needs to rephrase the question.

Did you have any role in the death of Shruti
Chatterjee?
No.

Don't say that. The words repeat in Suryakant's head.

Do you know who killed Shruti Chatterjee?
I don't know.

Where were you on the night of 11th October
around 11 PM?
I was at the terrace.

Suryakant realises that everything matches to what Sudarshan had narrated to him earlier.

Did someone come to your house on the night
of 11th October when you were on the terrace?
I am not sure. I don't remember.

Suryakant sits down. *What should I ask now?*

Did you kill…

He stops midway, turns off the video camera and comes out.

Back to square one.

Chapter 14
Gabhīra
(Mystery Deepens)

Chief's Cabin, CIU
November 10, 9:30 AM

Both Suryakant and Ajay are back in the room trying to absorb what had just happened.

"This can't be true, sir. I don't believe it," Suryakant says.

"An investigator should never get fixated on one idea. This seems to be a tricky case. You need to have an open mind."

The phone rings and Ajay picks it up. The operator says, "Sir, I have the Home Minister on line 2." Ajay presses line 2.

"Jai Hind, sir."

"Jai Hind. Ajay, what is the progress in the case of Shruti Chatterjee?"

"Sir, we are exploring multiple leads."

"This is the longest your team has taken to crack a case."

"Sir, the case is being investigated by Suryakant Singh. It's his first case."

Suryakant is taken aback by the remark.

"I want quick results. We need to say something to the media."

"Sir, as of now we don't have enough to charge Mr. Sudarshan."

"Are you clearing him?"

"No, sir. For now, we are letting him go. We are being extra careful as he is a *Padma Shri* recipient. We don't want to rush into anything. As I said, we have a few leads and we intend to explore them."

"Alright. Keep me posted."

"Right, sir."

The line gets disconnected. Ajay looks at Suryakant. "You need to act fast. There is a sense of unease among the higher ups. Get the other suspects ready. We got so fixated on one man, that we may have missed the others."

"Yes, sir."

"We are lucky that the Russian President is visiting the country and some important announcements are expected to be made. Media is busy there. This gives us some breathing space. Release Sudarshan for now."

"Yes, sir." Suryakant gets up and leaves the room.

❖❖❖

IR-1, CIU
November 10, 10 AM

Suryakant enters the room. He looks visibly dejected as compared to the first time Sudarshan saw him. Looking at the dull face of Suryakant, Sudarshan says, "Sir, what happened? When are you going to record my confession?"

"That will not be necessary. It was wrong on my part to use the death of your first wife to coerce a confession out of you. It was a mistake."

After a brief pause, Suryakant says, "You are free to go for now."

Sudarshan feels both relieved and surprised, "But if I may ask, what made you change your mind?"

"I realized my mistake. This is my first case and I was too eager to get results. But eventually better sense prevailed."

"But you won't say anything to my daughter and son."

"I am a man of my word," Suryakant replies in a loud and reassuring voice.

He means it. Sudarshan smiles. "There is something special about you. For some reason, I trust you. Very few police officers would have the guts to come in and say what you have just said."

After a pause, Sudarshan adds, "You and I are very much alike. Cut from the same cloth."

Suryakant doesn't understand why he is listening to him but Sudarshan's deep and thoughtful voice has some unexplainable enigma, so he lets the discussion go on.

Out of nowhere, Sudarshan asks, "Have you lost someone close to you?"

A bit surprised at the question, "Yes, someone very close," Suryakant replies softly.

He asks, "I noticed, the way you interrogated me, that you have an absolute hatred for criminals. And if I am not wrong, this must have developed due to your loss. Even I changed a lot when I lost my first wife Veena." Sudarshan pauses for a while and his eyes get wet. *A tragedy happens only once; you live it a million times in the head.*

"It was very hard for me. It turned me to spirituality and made me what I am today. I sense, the same is the case with you."

Sensing that Suryakant is absorbing his words, Sudarshan puts forth another surprise question, "Aren't you a Lord Shiva devotee?"

Suryakant is puzzled. *How does he know?* "Yes. But how do you know?"

"Even Shiva lost his wife Sati. A lot changes in you, when you lose someone close to you," Sudarshan explains, clearly avoiding answering the 'how'.

"But I am not an ardent Shiva devotee. When I was young, I liked many things about Lord Rama or Krishna and even Lord Hanuman."

"You don't get it. What's known as Hindu religion today, is actually a way of life. It gives us many Gods and Goddesses so that you can choose the God you like or who aligns with your thought process at any point of time in life. As we grow, our thinking changes, or to put it in a more appropriate manner, it develops. So does our choice of God or Goddess. Nothing is permanent except change."

Sudarshan has got Suryakant's attention and he wants to make full use of this opportunity. He continues, "It is this freedom, which makes it a beautiful way of life. An artist may choose Goddess Saraswati, a body builder may choose *pawan putra* Hanuman, an idealist - Lord Rama and a strategist - Lord Krishna. Similarly, those who are looking to destroy something like you and me, will look to Lord Shiva, the destroyer."

"What are you looking to destroy?" Suryakant responds sharply.

"Human suffering."

Suryakant stays quiet. As a critique, he responds, "You seem to be very spiritual in your thinking. But it is science that is providing answers to human suffering and not spiritual thinking."

Sudarshan smiles. "To me science and spirituality are the same. Two sides of the same coin. I always look at them as one. One needs the other. Let me ask, what is your educational background, officer?"

"I am a chemical engineer."

"That's good. So, I can ask you something." He picks up a pen and paper kept on the table. He sketches a chemical formula and asks, "What do you see?"

Suryakant takes the paper towards him and rotates it.

Suryakant looks at it for a while and then says, "It is

formula for Amobarbital chemical $C_{11}H_{18}N_2O_3$."

Sudarshan inverts the piece of paper. "You see a chemical formula but I see a Naṭarāja Statue. Our rational conscious mind is a great evolutionary asset. But sometimes it can be a limiting resource. One must outgrow it."

Did I hear it right or is this guy nuts? Suryakant has skepticism written all over his face. He does not even try to look at the page. But sensing the seriousness on the face of Sudarshan, he takes a re-look at the chemical formula. He tries to imagine the Naṭarāja pose.

After giving some time to Suryakant, Sudarshan says, "Humans have been given this gift of 'imagination'. Our ability to imagine and create fiction is what has led us to where we are today."

Sensing he has his ears, "Do you know how the structure of benzene C_6H_6 was discovered by German Chemist Friedrich August Kekulé?"

"No." Suryakant is still looking at the page.

Sudarshan takes the page back from him, turns it over and starts drawing, "Kekulé had two dreams at key moments of his work. In his first dream, in 1865, he saw atoms dance around and link to one another. He woke up and immediately began to sketch what he saw in his dream."

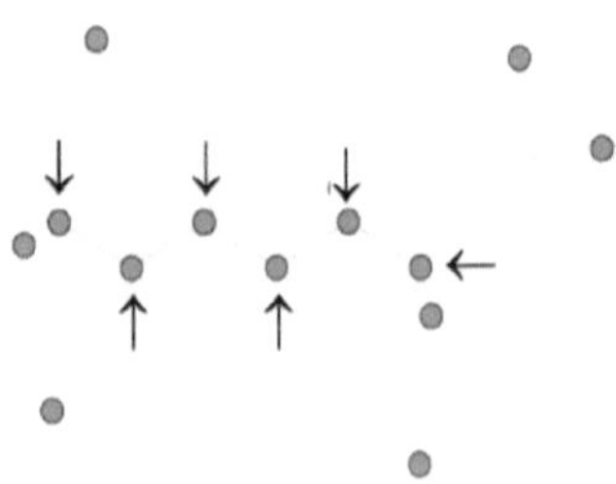

Later, he had another dream, in which he saw atoms dancing around and then forming a string, moving about in a snake-like fashion. This vision continued until the snake of atoms formed itself into an image of a snake eating its own tail. This dream gave Kekulé the idea of the cyclic structure of benzene."

"That's some dream, wouldn't you say? Pearls of knowledge are lying scattered all around us, sometimes hidden and at times in plain sight. Let me give you an example. You must have heard of Hanuman Chalisa. You must have heard the story that Hanuman ji had eaten the sun when he was a kid."

"Yes."

"The eighteenth *doha* (verse) in Hanuman Chalisa is *Juug Sahastra Yojana Par Bhanu, Leelyo Taahi Madhura Phala Jaanu.* This means that Sun (*Bhanu*) is at a distance of *Juug Sahastra Yojans* (Distance Unit in Veda). As per Hindu Vedic Literature,

1 Juug	=	12000
1 Sahastra	=	1000
1 Yojan	=	8 Miles
1 mile	=	1.6 km

Thus,

Distance	=	153,600,000 Kms

As per scientific calculations, the maximum distance between sun and earth is said to be 152,171,522 kms. Tulsidas was quite close in 15th century, won't you say?"

Suryakant is still grasping what he just heard.

When a wise teacher meets a worthy student, time seems to melt. Sudarshan seems to have forgotten all the tragic events of the last few days. He is in full flow now.

"Do you know about Arundhati-Vashishta star pair, which the married couple are asked to see?"

"I have heard that it is a common practice in South Indian marriages."

"Do you know why?"

Suryakant keeps quiet.

"In most twin star system, one star is stationary and the other rotates around it, while in the case of Arundhati and

Vashishta both rotate in synchrony. So as to say, that both husband and wife must do all things together and one must not merely rotate around the other, this ritual was made a part of the marriage ceremony." He draws a picture on the page.

"Thousands of years ago the ancient rishis could identify two tiny spots in the sky as a twin star system. They named it Arundhati-Vashishta, which are now commonly called as Alcor-Mizar stars in Ursa Major constellation (*Saptarishi*)."

Sudarshan looks at Suryakant and senses a bit of skepticism. But Sudarshan continues unabated, "You still think the knowledge is just spiritual and not scientific. Brhat Samhita was written around 6th century BC. It described the formation of rainbow in Chapter 35 as the multi-colored rays of the Sun, being dispersed in a cloudy sky, are seen in the form of a bow, which is called the rainbow. This was later proposed by Sir Issac Newton after nearly 2000 years."

"In fact, the same scripture describes formation of thunderbolt as well. Even in the Vedas, the seven colors of light are represented by seven horses of the Sun God."

Suryakant recollects the picture of Sun God in the

temple at his home.

It indeed has seven horses. He is right. Never knew what it signified.

"Have you heard the story of Kakudmi and his daughter Revati?"

Suryakant has a blank look on his face.

"Ok, let me narrate it for you. Bhagwat Puran in Verse 9.3 narrates the story of Kakudmi. Taking his own daughter, Revati, Kakudmi went to Lord Brahma in Brahmaloka, which is transcendental to the three modes of material nature and inquired about a husband for her. When Kakudmi arrived there, Lord Brahma was engaged in hearing musical performances by the Gandharvas. Therefore, Kakudmi waited, and at the end of the musical performances he offered his obeisance to Lord Brahma and then submitted his long-standing desire. After hearing his words, Lord Brahma, who is most powerful, laughed loudly and said to Kakudmi: 'O King, all those whom you may have decided within the core of your heart to accept as your son-in-law have passed away in the course of time.'

Twenty-seven Chatur Yugas have already passed. Those upon whom you may have decided are now gone, and so are their sons, grandsons and other descendants. You cannot even hear about their names. 'O King, leave here and offer your daughter to Lord Baladeva', who is still present.

Now let's do some maths,

1 Day of Brahmaloka is 1 Kalpa

1 Kalpa is equal to 1000 Chatur Yugas.

1 Chatur Yuga = 12,000 Deva years

1 Deva year = 360 Earth years

Thus, 1 second of Brahmaloka = 100,000 Earth years

Thus in 1 second of Brahmaloka, 1 Lakh Earth years pass. They listened to the music in Brahmaloka for 27 Chatur Yugas which works out to about 19.44 minutes. I leave it to you calculate how many earth years had already passed for Kakudmi and his daughter."

"What are you trying to convey?"

"Concept of time dilation and relativity. You don't see it?"

Suryakant recalls his father telling him that Kali Yuga equals 432,000 Human years. This means this Kali Yuga will just pass in 4.32 seconds for those from the Brahmaloka.

"You would be surprised to know that the Wachowski brothers who conceptualized the movie 'Matrix' were admittedly inspired by the Vedic thought among other things."

He continues, "We don't know; we might as well be in a *Matrix* as science fiction says or a *Maya jaal* as our Vedas say.

There are multiple references to the concept of relativity, time dilation, quantum physics and multiple universes in our scriptures. Modern Science is only now grappling with these questions in its infancy."

Suryakant has been bombarded with so many science and Vedic connections, that he can hardly speak any further.

"Some would say that this is over-interpretation of Vedic literature. They may be right, I don't know. But as I said, it is our 'imagination' that has made the difference for human civilization. You have to appreciate that a civilization could imagine all that thousands of years ago."

Suryakant is filled with a lot of cautionary admiration for Sudarshan. *This is no ordinary guy.* He starts to get up and leave.

Sudarshan says, 'When you first met me, you wanted to know the truth. This is my version of the truth. But it is not the only version of the truth. Truth is always multidimensional. To know the full truth of this case, you need to start asking the right questions. *Satya* (truth) does not lie in the answers, it lies in the right questions. May Lord Shiva show you the way."

Maybe I was wrong about him. Suryakant, still perplexed with the discussion, gets up to leave.

"You are free to go."

SI-3, CIU
November 10, 11:30 AM

Suryakant has been sitting in his room for more than an hour now. For quite some time Sudarshan's words keep creating a series of ripples in his mind, when the thought of the case ends his trance. The case is back to haunt him. He has to start all over again. *Who could be the other suspects?*

The case is not as straightforward as he has imagined. He takes out the CDR of Shruti Chatterjee again. She has many calls with Deepak Agarwal. Even Indu Mehra could be a suspect, he muses.

He opens the profile of Deepak Agarwal and Indu Mehra and begins to read. He takes a relook at the photograph of the crime scene to see if he has missed anything.

SSKA office is at Mayapuri. He decides to visit the office and have a word with Deepak Agarwal and Indu Mehra, when suddenly he gets a call on his cell phone from the nurse who takes care of his mother, Nandini Singh. *She only calls when there is an emergency.*

He picks up the phone. "Yes, is everything alright?"

"Aunty is complaining of chest pain. Please come quickly, sir."

"I will send an ambulance home. I am coming as soon as possible."

Suryakant calls Sir Ganga Ram Hospital near his home and asks them to send an ambulance to his residence. He rushes from his office without informing anybody.

Room, Sir Ganga Ram Hospital
November 10, 9 PM

The unusual smell of the corridor, strangers in pain, nervous faces of relatives and the beeping sound of equipment. A visit to a hospital is never pleasant, worse when someone close is admitted.

Suryakant is sitting with his mother in the hospital

room. She is stable now. Suryakant takes out his phone. There are six missed calls from Kritika. Suryakant is puzzled.

As he is about to call her back, his phone rings. It is Ajay Raj Singh. *He must be calling to inquire about his sister,* he thinks.

"Sir."

"How is Nandini?"

"She is stable. It was a mild heart attack but she is out of danger."

"I know this is the wrong time to tell you, but there is another death in the case you are investigating."

Suryakant's heart skips a beat. *Another death? Who could it be? I hope not Kritika.* The thought is almost instinctive.

"Who is it, sir?"

"It's Sudarshan. He is reported dead in his home. The daughter has reported the death. I need you to reach the crime scene immediately. Or should I send Vikram or Arif?"

He is shocked as hell. *Is it a murder or could it be a suicide? He didn't appear to be a suicidal kind of person.*

"No, sir. I will go. I am nearby."

"Alright. The forensics team is on the way. You need to go and take control of the situation. Our prime suspect is dead. This is going to be a big story. Lot of speculation will be there."

"Sir, I will leave immediately." he hangs up the phone. He says to himself: *the mess is getting messier. There is someone else. How deep does this rabbit hole go now!*

Suryakant wakes his mother up.

"Maa, I need to go to a crime scene, urgently. I will try to return in a couple of hours."

She knows it must be something very important, otherwise he wouldn't be telling her this. "It's alright. I will be fine. You go."

"I will speak with the Nurse and tell them to take care of you. I will ask one of my constables, Varsha to be here in case you need anything."

"There is no need for that. I will just sleep for the night."

Suryakant goes out of the room and makes a call to constable Varsha, asking her to reach the hospital room at the earliest. He leaves the hospital with a disturbed mind.

Chapter 15
AVACCHADA
(COVER)

Residence, Karol Bagh
November 10, 9:30 PM

Suryakant reaches the bungalow. There is already a media van standing and a reporter is saying something in front of the camera. He tries to hear what is being said,

There has been a sudden twist in the murder case of Shruti Chatterjee who was found dead two days ago under mysterious circumstances. Her husband Sudarshan Chatterjee was the prime suspect, but he was let go by police after questioning this morning. It is now learnt that Sudarshan Chatterjee is also dead. He was a Padma Shri recipient. The police are very tight lipped about the whole situation.

He avoids getting noticed by the reporter and quickly enters the house. He sees Kritika and Ayushman sitting on the sofa, crying. Their eyes look swollen. The servant Radhey is also standing at their side, sobbing. Satish Kapoor is sitting beside them, trying to console them. Police constables are standing outside a room. He can see the forensics team moving around. He takes out gloves from his pocket and wears them.

He enters the room and notices a dead body lying on the bed, the left side of body covered in blood. Nearly one-half of the bedsheet is soaked in blood. The second crime he gets to visit is in the same house with a lot of similarities. He says to himself, *It's the same murderer who killed both husband and wife. The two crimes have to be related. I wasted so much time focusing on the wrong guy. What did I miss?*

The photographer is done clicking photos. Suryakant goes close to the forensics guy and asks, "Is the murder weapon found?"

"Yes, sir. It was in the right hand of the victim. A broken glass from the photo frame of his dead wife. It is being inventoried."

"What is the expected time of death?"

"My guess would be around two hours back, i.e., between 7 to 8 PM."

He comes out of the room and goes and sits near Kritika.

"I am extremely sorry for your loss."

She shouts at him, "I told you he was innocent and you didn't believe me! If you had done your job properly, may be Baba would have been alive and the real criminal would have been behind the bars."

He understands her pain. *Within two days she has lost both her father and her mother.*

She instinctively reaches out for his hands for comfort and says, "Promise me, you will catch the culprit and put him behind bars."

Suryakant softly closes Kritika's hand into a fist and then places it on his heart, "I promise." A promise has been made again, the second one of his life.

"But I need your help. Tell me what happened." She calms her mind and starts to narrate. "We didn't know that you had released Baba from custody. He didn't call any of us. I was in a meeting with lawyer Mukesh Saini in the afternoon trying to convince him to take Baba's case. I returned around 8:30 PM. The front door was open, so I went inside. There was nobody at home. I went inside and saw…" She starts crying. "I tried calling you multiple times. When you did not pick up, I called Ajay sir informing him what I just saw. I then called Ayush, Satish uncle and Radhey. They came here just around half an hour back."

"Is there anything missing from the house?"

"Doesn't seem so."

Suryakant goes and talks with the forensics team. He goes around the house, including the terrace. He notices nothing out of the ordinary. After about an hour, he receives a call from Chief asking for an update. He leaves for the office.

Chief's Cabin, CIU
November 10, 11 PM

Suryakant reaches office to brief the boss. He is obviously still there. Suryakant enters his room. Ajay is sitting on his chair with a tense face and is listening to the Breaking News. He has already received a call from Mantriji.

"It's all over the news. They are making fun of us that the husband committed murder and we let him go. Now, he has committed suicide or has been murdered right under our nose. This is not good for us. Mantriji also called sometime back and he wants some solid result by tomorrow morning. You simply let him go and did not put a tail on him! How could you be so foolish?"

Foolish. It was you who asked me to let him go. "Sorry, sir, I saw no point in keeping an eye on him after we found out he was innocent. I also got a bit distracted by Maa's emergency." *Your bosses' mistake is your mistake in bureaucracy.*

"Only we knew he was innocent, not others." There is both desperation and disappointment in his voice.

Suryakant keeps listening.

"Do you think it's a suicide?"

"I highly doubt that, sir. He did not seem the suicidal type."

"But anyone who has lost his wife just two days back and is suspected to be the murderer will be in an unstable state of mind. Further, what you uncovered about the first wife could have worsened things for him mentally. Maybe he had some role in the death of his first wife. Eventually, it might have come out in the media, which would have led to his media trial and character assassination. He never would have liked his children to know such a thing. He would have feared about what may happen and, therefore, might have taken the easy way out. It looks like a suicide as well. I think it's in our best interest to term it as a suicide. It will be a win-win for all."

"What about the truth, sir? I have promised his daughter that I will get to the bottom of this."

"I understand Suryakant but I am under immense pressure."

"Sir, we know that he did not kill his wife. He passed the TS test."

"Suryakant there is something you need to know. You are family, so I am telling you. No one else can know."

Suryakant not knowing where this is going, keeps listening.

"Dr. Sudarshan Chatterjee was the inventor of this TS-108 drug. He created it. So, you know he could have beaten the TS test. Maybe he had an antidote developed or knew a way to beat it. He might have played all of us."

He was the inventor of this miracle drug! This is a big revelation to Suryakant.

That he shared this drug with him, means that he must be a very good friend of boss. And now the boss instead of investigating it deeply, is asking me to hush up the investigation. Boss kept it all covered up for so long, when this information was so crucial for the investigation. Something else is going on. He does not say anything further and leaves the room quietly.

Sudarshan neither made the TS public nor took any credit for it. This could have easily made him a fortune. In that moment, Suryakant's respect for Sudarshan knew no bounds. He indeed was a *Viśadātman* - a pure soul.

SI-3, CIU
November 10, 11:30 PM

Suryakant comes to his room and sits for a while. He

has a terrible headache. *Such a long day with so many developments.*

It is late. He remembers his mother. *Will think about this case tomorrow. Right now, I should go to the hospital.* He immediately gets up and leaves.

Room, Sir Ganga Ram Hospital
November 11, 00:30 AM

Lying on the guest bed in the room, Suryakant watches his mother Nandini sleeping. Many random thoughts enter his mind. He remembers his childhood and his father. Suddenly, that dreadful event in his life which changed everything for him comes to haunt him. He remembers how he was having a usual day at New York working in the office, when he received a call from his mother. He had talked to her just about two hours back.

"Hello, Maa."

"Surya, please come immediately beta," she starts to cry.

"What happened, Maa? Is everything alright? Where is Papa?"

"Your Papa has left us," she cried.

Suryakant's heart sinks and he collapses. His hands begin to shake.

"Don't say that, Maa." He too starts crying. This is the second time he has cried in his life as far as he remembers.

"How did it happen?"

"Someone stabbed him while returning home from the market...He was lying on the road, bleeding, for nearly 45 minutes...before someone noticed and reported it to the police." Crying gets louder. "He bled to death."

"I am coming, Maa."

His thoughts return to the room. Looking at Maa, he remembers how that day changed everything for him. He returned, never to go back again.

He misses his father, Pratap Singh, a lot. They were quite close. He was not just his father but his guru, a mentor and a friend. His father never wanted him to go to the USA, but he left nevertheless promising to return within two years. It was his fourth year in the USA, but his father had never reminded him of the promise. His eyes become wet. He dozes off with this thought.

News 360, Noida
November 11, 7 AM

TV in the room is playing a story

Welcome to the morning bulletin of News 360. Here are the headlines to get your day started.
The Russian President ...

Aditya is sitting in his room scanning through the internet, looking at the developing news story. The entourage of the Russian President has made the team work overnight.

Rakesh comes running. "Aditya, I have some inside news on the Sudarshan Chatterjee murder story. My sources have informed me that it is a suicide."

"What is your source?"

"It's right from the top."

"If it was a murder it would have been a better story."

Rakesh had expected such a response.

"He was Kritika's father."

"Yes, right. I see potential here."

"What do you mean?"

Raising his hands as if shooting a movie. "We can use her to do Part Two of her story. Part one was about Losers committing suicide. Part two can be about Achievers committing suicide. Who better than Kritika to give insights into her father's personal life?"

"You are a genius." *You are a bigger asshole than I thought.* Rakesh regrets giving him the news. He leaves the room and calls Kritika to give her a heads up on Aditya's devious plan.

Room, Sir Ganga Ram Hospital
November 11, 7:30 AM

A phone is buzzing. Suryakant wakes up with a startle. He notices the vibration of his phone. He has kept the phone on silent mode so as not to wake his mother up. He takes it out and finds that the call is from Kritika. He presses the green symbol.

"Yes, Kritika. Is everything alright?"

"I want to meet you. It's urgent."

"Actually, it's not a good time. I am at Sir Ganga Ram Hospital. My mother is admitted here. Can we meet later in the day?"

"Please…just meet for me for five minutes. I will come over to the hospital. It's nearby."

Suryakant looks at his watch. Sees it's around 7:30 AM. *It's so early but she is still insisting. Might be something important.* "Alright, I will meet you at the reception lobby. Call me when you get here."

"Thank you for your consideration. I should be there

in 15 minutes' tops." She hangs up abruptly.

His mother is still asleep. It's a cold morning. He gets up and goes to the bathroom. He quickly brushes his teeth and combs his hair. Some time is spent in choosing the shirt that he is going to wear. He puts on a pair of jeans and then a carefully selected maroon sweatshirt. He picks up a jacket and goes downstairs.

Lobby, Sir Ganga Ram Hospital
November 11, 8 AM

"Hello."

"You want coffee?"

"Yes, a cup of coffee will help."

They both move towards an A2B coffee vending machine nearby and take two coffees. They sit down on the sofa in the lobby.

"Tell me what it is about."

"I heard that my father's death is being treated as a suicide."

Suryakant frowns. This is unusual. He chooses his words with care. "What makes you think so? As far as I know all possibilities are being explored right now."

"My boss Adi at 'News 360' says that the police officials have informally termed it as a suicide. They are going to put it on the morning news. The media is going to go ahead with this version of the story."

Could it be the boss leaking this news? He had to give the Home Minister an update in the morning. He would like it if the media was going this way.

"I feel it's just a rumor. The post-mortem hasn't been

done yet. You know the media more than I do and how unreliable it's sources are."

"I know it's a murder. Baba cannot commit suicide and leave me and Ayush alone. I just came down to implore you to make sure to get to the bottom of this. This suicide story is a big 'cover up'. I know my father was doing something very important. He never used to discuss office work with us, but Mumma told us that father is doing some important work. And someone has used this opportunity to silence him. You must have met him, what do you feel?"

Suryakant hesitates. *I know what that important work was. But I am not sure who all actually know about it. It seems that at least Kritika doesn't know.* Suryakant wants to keep quiet but then feels the urge to reassure her. "Trust me. I promised you, I will get to the bottom of this. And I intend to keep my promise." He keeps his hand on her hand in a reassuring manner.

She moves her hand away.

Too soon. He thinks to himself, *This is not the right time.* Trying to change the topic, he asks, "Can you think of anyone who could have hurt your father?"

"I can't be sure, but Deepak uncle and Baba used to have many arguments. Deepak uncle is very money minded, and he wasn't happy with Baba's philanthropic nature. Moreover, I saw him that day in front of ACP Ashutosh and noticed how he tried to imply that Baba and Mumma had disagreements over the house. It was such a big lie."

"Are you sure that it was a lie?" he asked.

"Mumma and Baba were not that type to fight over money. If Baba wanted to sell or mortgage the house, he would have definitely discussed with Mumma before. And Mumma would have told me." Suryakant wonders if she really knew her father. He has kept many secrets from all of them.

But she is right, *Deepak is a potential suspect.* He remembers that the phone records showed Shruti and Deepak had exchanged many calls.

He asks, "How close were your mother and Deepak?"

"What do you mean?"

"Just asking if he had any role in your mother's death as well. The two may be connected, you know."

"I can with certainty say that they were not close friends or anything like that. In fact, I feel they hardly knew each other."

Is she hiding something or maybe she doesn't know? Because the call records paint a different picture.

"Your mother was a homemaker. Right?"

"Yes, but she used to teach until a couple of years ago when she quit due to her health problems. She also used to paint. But of - late she did very little of that."

"Okay."

They both realize that their coffees have got over a while back. Like two broken souls, they both need some company, someone to talk to. He likes her very much but doesn't know how she feels. *She lost her father, just like I had lost mine. The police department failed me but I will not fail her,* he says to himself.

Kritika looks at her wristwatch, "It's already 8:30 AM. I should get going. Ayush will be waiting at home."

"Should I drop you?" He wants to drop her.

"No, I came driving my own car. I can go. You need to stay with your mother. Sorry I didn't even ask about her. What happened? I mean, how is she?"

"That's okay. She is fine. Nothing serious. You have a lot on your mind already. Please go home and take some rest."

She thanks him once again and leaves. He keeps on looking at her but she does not turn back.

Suddenly, the case feels personal now.

Room, Sir Ganga Ram Hospital
November 11, 8:45 AM

Suryakant returns to the room and sees that his mother is awake, and nurse is doing the morning check-up. The nurse leaves after five minutes.

Nandini asks, "Where did you go?"

"It's the case, I am working on, Maa. Nothing is what it seems. I am so confused."

Nandini gives a smile to him, "Come here."

He goes and sits on a chair near the bed. He keeps his head near her and covers his face. She puts her hands on his hair trying to calm his mind, "What's wrong Surya?"

Suryakant is looking the other way. Yesterday's discussion with Sudarshan and his death now, has brought back the memories of his father. For the first time since his death, he feels as if his Papa is talking to him. Finally, he gathers the strength to ask, "Maa, I never asked. Did Papa ever say anything when I did not return from the US? I never got to meet him. Was that my punishment?" He hides his face.

She instantly understands what was bothering him. They have never talked about it. "Surya, you are the best son, we could have ever got. Your Papa loved you more than anything in this world. He could have never thought of punishing you. I still remember when you were born, the Guruji (priest) who made your *kundali,* said that your son is going to go very far. And you know what your Papa asked."

"How far? Will he be the first to reach Mars?"

Suryakant laughs.

"He wanted you to touch the heights no one has scaled before, even if it meant you staying away from him."

"Surya, I won't lie to you. Your father was an honest police inspector and he always dreamed that his son would become what he couldn't, an IPS officer. He did not want you to leave. But he also did not want you to be chained to his dreams."

"Guruji had also said that you were special because you had the gift. Your heart will always be at the right place. You will have the strength to do what no ordinary person will be able to. And you will have to make a difficult, life-altering choice."

"What choice, Maa?"

"I think you have already made that choice, Surya, by returning to India, leaving all behind. Like Lord Krishna left Vrindavan never to return, because he had to fight the Kurukshetra war. Destiny wanted you here."

"Your Papa had told me to always support you in whatever you decide. He will always be there to guide you. Remember that." He now knew that Papa had always been there to cover for him and would always be there to guide him.

Suryakant closed his eyes. *I have kept the promise. I have fulfilled your dream.* In that moment, Suryakant, the son finds the closure he had been searching for all this while.

❖❖❖

Chapter 16
Talāsh
(Hunt)

SI-3, CIU
November 11, 11 AM

Suryakant returns to work. He is relieved that his mother has been discharged and is out of danger. That is one problem less. *A complex case is still at hand.*

He calls Brijesh. "Has the post-mortem report of Mr. Sudarshan come?"

"No, sir. Dr. Ramakant Joshi, our forensics expert, is not well. Maybe he will come by tomorrow."

"And is there any progress on the case file of the first wife?"

"No, sir. They are unable to locate it. I spoke to them this morning as well."

"Ok." He cuts the call.

I need some answers from Ajay sir on TS-108. He gets up and goes straight to the boss's room.

Chief's Cabin, CIU
November 11, 11:20 AM

"May I come in, sir."

"Yes, Suryakant. Come in. Any update on the case?"

"No, sir, I am still awaiting the post-mortem report."

"Ok."

"Sir, if you permit, may I ask a question?"

"What kind of question?"

"Sir, this TS-108…do we have the formula or is it lost after the death of Sudarshan?"

"As of now, we have it in sufficient quantity to test it on 100 suspects. Sudarshan had developed it and given it to us without anyone knowing about it. That was our little arrangement. A secret for both sides."

"But why did he give it you secretly?"

"I had handled the investigation of his first wife's death and we got close. We used to discuss how suspects got away so easily, and how the police force was handicapped. Many a time the investigation was poor, and we didn't have all the evidence. Nobody ever tells the complete truth. An investigator only looks at parts of a canvas but never gets to look at the complete picture."

Suryakant listens patiently.

"The situation further compounds when lawyers exploit loopholes in investigation. Our judicial process also works at a snail's pace. It is nearly impossible to get a conviction."

After a brief pause, he continues, "The balance in the society was tipping on the side of evil, in the words of

Sudarshan. So, when he developed this drug, he wanted it to be used secretly to destroy criminals. He believed that the drug would last only if it remains a secret. The day it is known to the public, others will either reverse-engineer it or someone will develop an antidote, rendering it useless. It had to be used, secretly. So, I came up with the idea of CIU. The government thinks we are just using coercion, lie detector test, narco test, etc. without consent. That's what we got it approved for. Mind you, we still don't cut any corners on investigation. TS-108 just tips the balance back in our favor."

"Sir, what is its future now, do we have the formula? Can we develop it in-house?"

"We don't have the formula." He sighs and then says, "This is one more reason I brought you in to CIU."

Suryakant gets shocked. He realizes that he is a chemical engineer and had worked in a research Lab at the US for three years, developing such drugs before returning to India and joining IPS. *This was 'the' reason, everything else was an eyewash.*

"I would have introduced you to him sooner but all this shit happened. In fact, we had talked a lot about you. Can you develop this drug?"

You talked to him about me? Now he begins to understand how Sudarshan knew so much about him during their discussion.

He thinks for a while and replies, "Sir, I have friends working in research labs. I can take their assistance and try to work out its chemical composition and reverse engineer the formula. But it is going to take time to guess the ingredients and chemical processes to make it."

"That's good news. Get right on it. Now you understand why we need to close this case quickly. The more we investigate, more are the chances that the secret will come out. And our priority should be to get this TS-108 developed secretly in-house."

The engineer in Suryakant asks, "Are there any known side-effects of this TS-108?"

"Sudarshan said that it was still in an experimental stage, but initial trials had shown no side-effects. That's why he gave us only 200 samples to start with. Even we haven't noticed any side-effects so far. Though, he cautioned against its use more than once on any person within a month or so."

He further adds, "I also want you to go through the inventoried material - his computer, laptop, diary, anything relevant seized from his house, to see if it contains any notes on this TS-108."

Suryakant is able to connect the dots now. But he does not agree on closing the case quickly. *Is the boss telling the truth or he is just trying to cover it up?*

"Sir, but at least we should solve his case. We owe this much to him, otherwise, we won't be able to live with ourselves."

"You are right. We owe this much to him," Ajay nods.

"So, what is your next step?"

"Sir, I am thinking of putting Mr. Deepak Agarwal, CFO of the company through TS test. Sudarshan's daughter thinks he could be a suspect. There were differences over financial matters. I need your authorization to put Mr. Deepak Agarwal through TS test."

Ajay thinks for a while and then answers, "You have my authorization."

❖ ❖ ❖

SI-3, CIU
November 11, noon

Suryakant enters his room. He had gone to Chief's room to get some answers, but returned with more questions.

Bureaucrats tend to make rules for others and exceptions for themselves. Suryakant is unable to trust Ajay sir. *He got me into CIU because of my educational background. He wanted to use me to meet his own end. But from his perspective, it made sense. I am family to him, so I can be trusted. And he knew why I joined IPS and am motivated for an organization like CIU. Yesterday, he wanted it to be called suicide. At least today he agreed to continue with the investigation of the case.*

His thoughts are eating him up. He picks up a paper and starts to write:

Victims	-	Shruti & Sudarshan Chatterjee
Family	-	Kritika and Ayushman
Business	-	Deepak Agarwal, Indu Mehra, anybody else like the secretary??

He thinks for some time and then writes

Friend	-	Satish Kapoor, Radhey

He again thinks for a while and then adds one more name to the list

Ajay Raj Singh

He picks up his intercom and dials 212, "Mukesh,

bring in Mr. Deepak Agarwal for questioning and get him seated in IR-2."

"Right, sir," he says.

He hangs up the phone.

He starts to think - *Deepak is the CFO of the company. He is money minded. If he had come to know about the drug, he might have tried to mint money from it. He tried to misguide the wife's death investigation by leading us to Sudarshan by slipping in the fact that the husband and wife were having problems. If Sudarshan had gone to jail, he would have got control over the company. Running it the way he wants. That's a motive.*

He remembers that wife's call record had shown many calls with Deepak. He takes out the call record and starts going through it again. He opens the system and goes to the folder where the CDRs are kept in digital form. He starts looking at the common calls between Deepak and Shruti. It is a huge data to grasp.

Kritika said they hardly knew each other, or did they? The CDR says something else!

He remembers Vikram's words that hard evidence does not lie.

He takes out a plain paper and writes serial number one with Deepak Agarwal in front of it. He folds the paper and keeps it in his pocket.

IR-2, CIU
November 11, 2:30 PM

The door to IR-2 opens. Suryakant enters along with Arif. Arif hands him the bottle and signals him to go inside.

As Suryakant enters, Deepak says, "Why have I been

called here? Am I a suspect?"

"No, sir, you have been called just for some questions."

"Questions like?"

"How well did you know Shruti Chatterjee?"

"What do you mean? She was Sudarshan's wife. We were just friends."

"Just friends or a good friend?"

Deepak gets up from the seat angrily. "I don't like these kinds of questions. I want my lawyer to be with me. You can't ask me such questions."

"Calm down, sir. You don't have to answer them if you don't want to. Please have some water." Pushing the bottle towards him.

Deepak picks up the bottle and starts drinking it.

"You had told ACP Ashutosh that the company was going through a rough patch financially and Sudarshan wanted to sell his house. Did Shruti agree with him?"

Deepak thinks for a moment, drinks some more water and then replies, "I don't know."

After a few seconds, he goes into sleep. Suryakant quickly turns on the video recorder and starts the procedure.

```
What is your name?
Deepak Agarwal.

Did you kill Sudarshan Chatterjee or Shruti
Chatterjee?
No.

Did you have any role in the murder of
Sudarshan Chatterjee or Shruti Chatterjee?
No.
```

You had made many calls to Shruti's cell phone. What was the reason for so many calls?
I normally called on Shruti's cell phone to speak with Sudarshan due to network issues on his cell phone number.

How wrong was my interpretation of the facts! Suryakant realises, feeling a bit ashamed of his assumptions, that this possibility never came to his mind.

Do you know anything about TS-108 drug?
No.

Utterly disappointed he stops the camera and then comes out.

Arif tells him, "So even this suspect is out. Maybe the wife's death was an accident and the husband's was suicide. Unfortunately, we can't use this TS-108 on the dead. A sad end for the family."

Suryakant cautiously responds, "Yes, sir. It looks like that."

They both leave the room. A guard is sitting outside. Arif tells him, "You can ask him to leave. Say something came up, so sir had to go."

Chapter 17

RATI

(DESIRE)

SI-3, CIU
November 11, 3 PM

Suryakant is sitting looking at a montage he has made on the whiteboard in his office. There are not too many options left now. *Sitting in this room, I am not going to look beyond my blind spots. Maybe I should visit Sudarshan's office and look around. It might throw up something. Indu Mehra also needs to be questioned.*

Deciding not to tell the boss or anyone where he is going, he picks up his aviators and goes down. His driver is waiting.

"Take me to Mayapuri."

SSKA Office, Mayapuri
November 11, 4 PM

Suryakant shows his ID to the security at the gate and tells him that he has come to meet Indu Mehra. The security guard makes a call and then asks Suryakant to go inside.

He slowly starts walking in the corridor. There are nearly ten employees on this floor. There is a door with the name of Sudarshan Chatterjee. He goes towards the room. There is a secretary sitting outside the cabin.

Suryakant reads the name on the desk, "Priya Mehta."

"Good evening, Miss Priya. I am Special Investigator Suryakant Singh. I am investigating the death of Mr. Chatterjee."

"Its Dr. Chatterjee," she interjects.

"Sorry. My apologies. Since how long you have been his secretary?"

"Nearly five years now."

"That's a long time. So, you must know him quite well. Do you have your suspicion on anyone or have any kind of information that might help the investigation?"

"Not sure if I can be of any help, sir."

"Do you think it was a suicide?"

"I don't think Dr. Chatterjee was capable of committing suicide. He was a very strong person mentally. Very ethically and spiritually driven. Never mad for profits. No matter how much Mr. Deepak Agarwal and Dr. Indu Mehra disagreed, he never relented."

"Were Dr. Indu Mehra and Dr. Chatterjee close?"

She keeps quiet.

Sensing he had hit on something, Suryakant pushes her a little more. "These personal questions are very important from the investigation point of view. I am sure you would want the murderer to be caught."

"Dr Indu Mehra was divorced recently and I think she was trying to get close to him."

"What do you mean 'close to him'?"

"See, I am a woman. I know when a woman likes someone. She would always look at the mirror before entering his room. The perfume, the lipstick, the way she looked at him - the signs were everywhere!"

Priya continues, "She is someone anyone would fall for. Beauty, brains, sensuality all wrapped into one."

"But what about Dr. Chatterjee? Did he also reciprocate?"

"That's difficult to know. But if you ask me, Dr. Chatterjee was never interested in her. He loved Shruti ma'am a lot. Dr. Mehra had undergone a divorce around six months back. For the last few months, I had noticed Dr. Chatterjee giving her attention, maybe to comfort her and many times he left with Dr. Mehra, which he had never done earlier."

Why did I not come to this office earlier?

Suryakant thanks Priya Mehta for her inputs. She asks whether all the information that she has shared will be kept confidential. His smile and a few words, assure her. He then goes inside Sudarshan's cabin and begins to look around. There are three photos kept on the table and some office papers lie scattered. One of the photos is of his family, the other with his office colleagues and the third one appeared to be from Sudarshan's college days. There are six persons in the photograph: four males and two females. He recognizes Sudarshan and his first wife Veena among them. There is a big Nataraja statue kept on the side table. Looking at statue, Suryakant breaks into a warm smile.

On the wall, there is the *Padma Shri* award framed and put up right in the center. The drawers and cupboards have general office related papers. There is nothing out of the ordinary. There is neither any desktop nor any laptop in the room. He comes out of the room. He knows where he needs to go next.

Indu's Cabin, SSKA
November 11, 4 PM

Indu Mehra already knows that Suryakant has come. The security had informed her. Prashant is sitting on the sofa in her room and is restless.

"Mom, should I leave?"

"No, that might raise suspicion. I don't know what Priya might have told him."

"I am scared."

"Don't worry. Just keep quiet. I will do all the talking."

"But still if he asks me anything?"

"I will handle it. We don't have to worry if we don't say anything more than what is required."

She stands and takes a look in the mirror in her room. As Suryakant is about to reach the cabin, she goes out of the room to receive him.

She is dressed in a creamy white salwar-kameez, which matches her complexion. She is wearing high heels and black bangles. The clothes are adding grace to her already God gifted features. There is a small black *bindi* on her forehead and nude lipstick on her lips. Her walk is as elegant as a swan floating on water. As she approaches, the smell of her perfume leaves him breathless. Suryakant is floored by her beauty.

She confidently offers a handshake. "How are you, officer?"

Suryakant responds in kind. His voice breaks for a second, "Ahem…I am fine. How are you?" *She is indeed a beauty to behold.*

"Difficult to say. Lost so much at a personal level in just a week."

They both go inside the room. Suryakant notices Prashant. *I have seen him before somewhere.*

Indu introduces, "This is my son Prashant."

Prashant stands up and says, "Good morning, sir. Ehhh… I mean Good evening, sir."

Suryakant walks and extends his hand. "Good evening." The face looks familiar to him. "I think we have met before."

"No, sir. I have a very common face," he lies and smiles. *It is good that he doesn't remember!*

Indu interrupts the discussion, "Please have a seat, officer." They both move and sit on the sofa. "Would you like to have some tea or coffee?"

"No, thank you."

"Tell me, how can I help you, sir?"

He feels that it is better to start from some other topic and slowly move into the real reason for the visit. "So, what does this company do exactly?"

"We mainly do research and development of new chemicals and drugs."

"What kind of chemicals and drugs?"

"Mostly drugs to enhance human capabilities and to fight diseases. Sudarshan was very knowledgeable. For instance, recently our team developed a formula for the corona virus."

"That sounds interesting. The company must be making good money for developing such products."

"Not really. Sudarshan never believed in commercialization of products. He used to get the product patented and then used to license it to other companies for mass production for a very nominal charge. His only condition was that these savings should be passed to the end consumer. He wanted the society to benefit from his research."

"If he wanted, he could have become very rich. But that was never his aspiration. He was a renowned researcher before he started the company and had received the Padma Shri for his contribution a few years back."

Very honorable man. Suryakant thinks to himself.

"And you agreed with his approach?"

"Yes. We were friends since college. He was the brain behind this company, I joined this company only because of him. We are lost without him now."

Suryakant could notice her eyes getting teary. "Are you married Dr. Mehra?"

"I was. But I am divorced now."

"I am sorry to hear that."

"You don't have to be sorry. It was mutual."

"How many children do you have?"

"Prashant is my only son," she says pointing her face towards Prashant.

"What does he do?"

"He is in college. In fact, he is a very good friend of Sudarshan's son, Ayushman, just like we were in college." She felt quite happy saying that.

Indu looks at a photo frame kept on her table. Suryakant recognizes the photo. It is the same photograph he saw in Sudarshan's cabin. He moves and picks up the photograph. "Who are these?"

"This is a photograph of our college days. I am on the extreme left. Next to me are Sudarshan and his first wife Veena. Next to them are Ashutosh, Ratan and Satish. We were very good friends in those days. Ashutosh is no more. Ratan is a big businessman based in Mumbai. Satish, I think is a researcher in Bangalore. Except Sudarshan, it's been ages since I have met or even talked with Ratan or Satish. Now even he is gone." The heaviness in her voice could easily be felt.

Keeping the photograph back on table, Suryakant says, "Prashant, can you excuse us for some time? I have to ask your mother some questions."

"Yes, sir." Prashant is very much relieved. He gets up and starts to leave the room. As he is walking, his phone rings. The ringtone is very peculiar. Suryakant recognizes it is from an old American TV series Dexter. Prashant quickly silences it and sees the caller. It's from Vaidehi. He goes out of the room and takes the call.

Suryakant continues, "Ma'am, I need to ask some personal and procedural questions. Please don't get me wrong."

"Sure, please go ahead. I would like to help."

"Where were you on the night of the death of Shruti Chatterjee?"

"I was at home."

"Were you alone at home?"

"Yes."

"Can anyone confirm that?"

"I need to think. I reached home around 7 PM. Had dinner and then slept by 9 PM. Difficult to get anyone to confirm that I was sleeping," she jokes.

"Where were you on the day of death of Dr. Sudarshan Chatterjee?"

"Once again, I was at home. I took the day off with so much going around."

"Can anyone confirm that?"

"I am afraid I was alone at home. But I was not even aware that Sudarshan had been released and he would be at home."

"Your phone record shows that you had spoken with Sudarshan in the evening?"

Her face suddenly turns pale. She says in a panicky voice, "Hmm…yes, I remember now, I had spoken to him for a minute. But he wanted to be alone."

"What did you talk about?"

"Nothing. It was a general talk."

"Please pardon me asking this but were you and Sudarshan more than friends?"

She gets outraged. "What kind of question is this? And how is this relevant?"

"Sorry, Ma'am, but this is a murder investigation. All these questions matter in such cases."

She doesn't respond anything further. After a while, she says, "Is there anything else, officer?"

"No, ma'am, thank you for your time. And sorry again."

Suryakant leaves knowing he has his new suspect and adds the name of Dr. Indu Mehra to the list.

Meanwhile, Prashant is talking to Vaidehi outside the cabin.

"Hi Vaidehi."

"Hi Prashant. Where are you? You haven't come to college for the last few days."

"Yes, I didn't feel like coming to college due to the recent events."

Her voice saddens, "Yeah. Ayushman hasn't answered my calls or messages. How is he holding up? Have you met him? My father won't let me go to his house."

"The last few days have been very rough for all of us…I mean…I mean for him. I was with him yesterday. He needs time."

"Yes, I understand."

"Please ask him to reply to my messages."

"I will. And don't worry, you can call me whenever you feel like."

"Thanks, Prashant, for everything."

"No need to say thanks. I am always there for you."

Prashant hangs up the phone. He is still nervous and anxiously waits for Suryakant to leave.

Chief's Cabin, CIU
November 11, 5:30 PM

"Sir, I want to put Dr. Indu Mehra to the TS test."

"What makes her a suspect?"

"Sir, she claimed to be alone at her home at the time of death of both Dr. and Mrs. Chatterjee, but she has no one to confirm this fact. The secretary to Dr. Sudarshan Chatterjee told me that the relationship between Dr. Chatterjee and Dr. Mehra could have been more than just friendship. According to her, she had a thing for Sudarshan. This happened right after her divorce and things between Shruti and Sudarshan Chatterjee were not at their best maybe due to financial trouble and house dispute. Moreover, she is the last one to have spoken with Sudarshan. And the phone record shows that she was travelling at that time."

"The no alibi thing is interesting but the other thing is just hearsay. You don't know the equations between the two ladies. Women can say just anything about each other. Can you get anybody else to confirm this?"

"No, sir. But her reaction was extreme when I asked her about the phone call and her relationship with Sudarshan. Just to rule her out, I want your approval to conduct the TS test on her."

"She may have a motive to kill Shruti if she wanted Sudarshan in her life, but why would she kill him?"

"Maybe Sudarshan came to know about it."

"It sounds too far-fetched. But you have my approval,

just to rule her out."

"Thank you, sir."

"It's late for today. Question her tomorrow morning. Call her on the ground that we need her fingerprints."

"Right, sir."

IR-1, CIU
November 12, 10 AM

Arif and Suryakant both are standing looking at the suspect. Never before has Suryakant seen Arif look at a suspect with such amorous eyes.

"Are you ready?" Arif asks intently.

"Yes, sir."

Arif hands over the bottle to Suryakant. "Hope you are right this time."

"Thank you, sir." Suryakant takes the bottle and goes inside the room.

"Good morning, Dr. Mehra."

There is no response.

"Sorry Ma'am but please don't take it personally. In an investigation, we are forced to ask all kinds of questions, just to get to the truth."

"You have no rights to ask personal questions."

Suryakant places the bottle in front of her.

"Ma'am, it maybe personal to you, but in many cases personal relations are the cause for murder. We can't ignore anything. But if you don't want to answer such questions, no further questions in this regard will be asked." He smiles.

"Let us get this over with, quickly." She picks up

the bottle and drinks it. Suryakant pretends to open the fingerprint kit he has brought.

Dr. Indu Mehra goes to sleep. Suryakant turns on the video recorder.

```
What is your name?
```
Indu Mehra.

```
Did you kill Sudarshan Chatterjee or Shruti
Chatterjee?
```

Suryakant desperately hopes for a 'YES'.

No.

```
Did you have any role in the murder of
Sudarshan Chatterjee or Shruti Chatterjee?
```
No.

Suryakant's disappointment knows no bounds.

```
Did your relationship with Sudarshan
Chatterjee involve sex?
```
No.

```
Where were you around the time of death of
Shruti Chatterjee?
```
I was at home.

```
Where were you in the evening of the day
when Sudarshan Chatterjee died?
```
I was at home.

Everything she said was correct. She is not the one!

```
Do you know anything about TS-108?
```
No.

Suryakant thinks for a while. He remembers that the question needs to be specific. He had missed this during questioning of Deepak Agarwal. He rephrases

Did you know of any Truth Serum being developed by Sudarshan Chatterjee?
Yes.

Arif folds his hands and begins to listen carefully.

What do you know about the Truth Serum?
It was an idea of Sudarshan's, and it remained an idea. We discussed it for quite some time but it was not leading anywhere. So, it was dropped.

Suryakant thinks for a while and then asks,

Was an antidote of Truth Serum also being developed?
Yes.

Who was developing it?
I was developing it.

Was Sudarshan also developing an antidote to Truth Serum?
No. He was in fact against the idea of an antidote.

Why were you developing an antidote when the Truth Serum itself was not developed?
Deepak and I thought that it will help us make a lot of money, in case the Truth Serum gets developed in the future. In any case, such an antidote would have helped against

Lie detector, narco and other such tests. There is a lot of demand for the product. We were developing it secretly.

Have you been successful in developing the antidote to Truth Serum?
No.

Arif enters the room. "The time is up; we need to close it before she wakes up."

"But I have a few more questions? We need to know if someone else knows about development of Truth Serum or if someone was paying them to develop the antidote."

"It's late. We can't take any risk."

He stops the video recorder and picks up the bottle and takes Suryakant out with him.

"They don't know about TS-108 as Sudarshan kept the secret quite well and the antidote is not yet developed. So, it does not matter."

Suryakant realizes that Arif also knows about Sudarshan being the inventor of TS-108. *So, boss lied to me when he said no one else knows about it.*

I think I know my next suspect.

Chapter 18
Patana
(Fall from Grace)

SI-3, CIU
November 12, 10:45 AM

No one can be trusted. Suryakant takes out the list and strikes-off the name Indu Mehra. He moves to his next name in the list now 'Ajay Raj Singh'.

What all do I know? Suryakant says to himself.

1. *He lied that I have been absorbed in CIU for 'investigation', when he clearly had other plans.*

2. *He lied that only we both know that Sudarshan was the inventor of TS-108. Arif also knows. What about Vikram?*

3. *He tried to hush up the investigation as a suicide.*

4. *He never mentioned about the death of Sudarshan's first wife until I found out. He did not let me ask Sudarshan about the death of his first wife.*

5. *Vikram and Arif are experienced investigators. Instead he picked me, an amateur, to investigate this case, so that he can be in control.*

6. *Why did Sudarshan choose / trust him enough to share TS-108? Did boss help in the cover-up of the 'murder' of the first wife? The case file is missing!*

7. *Maybe he was misusing TS-108 and Sudarshan wanted to stop him, this led him to murder Sudarshan. To cover it up, he got the case assigned to CIU.*

He could sense a storm building up in his mind. The wind of this storm was fanning the anger in him. The image of Ajay sir was getting shattered with every passing second. The more he thought, the more he got convinced.

Is this the cover-up Kritika was talking about? I need to talk to her once. Maybe she knows something.

He picks up the phone and calls Kritika.

"Hi, Suryakant sir."

"Hi, please call me just Suryakant. Can we meet? I need to discuss something."

"We can discuss it on the phone or video call if its urgent."

"No, it's better to discuss in person."

She realizes it is something serious. "Where should I come?"

"Don't trouble yourself. I will come over. Your coming here might raise suspicion. I will be at your home in an hour."

"Ok."

Suryakant hangs up the phone and leaves.

Residence, Karol Bagh
November 12, 11:30 AM

Suryakant presses the doorbell. Kritika comes and opens the door.

"Hi."

"Please come in."

"How are you holding up?"

"It's been very hard. To lose everything so suddenly. We were so happy together. Why would someone come and spoil everything!" she starts to cry.

Suryakant holds her hand. This time she doesn't pull her hand away.

Maybe I should tell her about TS-108 drug developed by her father. Maybe not. Some secrets should stay secret, Suryakant rationalizes to himself.

"You have to stay strong. You both have a long life ahead."

He had to let go of her hand. But for the first time, he felt something from her side too.

"You told me that your father was working on something important and you suspected a cover-up. Do you remember anything which can help us?"

She feels happy that her words have been given importance.

"There is nothing in particular that I can remember."

"I have learnt that your father developed something very important and it was secretly being used by the government. Do you have any idea?"

"He never used to talk about work. He was not exactly happy that I did not join his beloved company. But he was not the type who would complain or force someone… specially me to do something against my wishes."

"Do you remember if he had received any threats?"

"I don't recall Baba or Mumma mentioning about any threat."

"Is there anything missing from home?"

"Nothing valuable seems to be missing."

"Not items like jewelry or money. Any laptop or computer or notes of your father. If he was working on something important secretly then those things are more valuable than the traditional valuables. Think carefully."

She gets up and walks to the 'study' room of her father. She starts to look around. His laptop and cell phone phone have been seized by the police. She carefully looks at the table. Then she remembers.

"Baba had a diary…" On not finding it where it was normally kept, she says, "Maybe that was also seized by the police."

"I have checked the seized items inventory, there is no mention of any diary there."

"Then that diary is missing."

"I may know who might be behind it."

"Who?"

"Will tell you later. Just don't tell anyone about the diary. I don't want you getting into any trouble."

She nods.

Suryakant leaves in a hurry.

SI-1, CIU

November 12, 1 PM

"May I come in, sir."

"Yes, Suryakant. Please come in."

Vikram sees anxiousness on Suryakant's face.

"Sir, I want to ask you a question?"

"Yes, ask me anything."

"Do you know where this TS-108 drug came from? I mean who developed it?"

"That only the boss knows. When he recruited us, he told us to never ask or even try to find out how we got this TS-108. He said if it comes out, then it will be difficult to keep it a secret. It made sense as well. So, I never tried to find out."

"Right, sir. I agree with you. Do you think Arif sir knows about the developer?"

"I am not sure. He might. He is quite close to boss. The boss trusts him with the custody of TS-108. Even I don't have access to that room."

"But why do you ask?"

"Sir, if I told you that the developer might be dead, do you think anyone from CIU could be behind it?"

Developer might be dead. "How do you know developer is dead?"

"Sir, the developer was none other than Sudarshan. It appears to be a big conspiracy, the way both husband and wife were found dead."

This is news. Why hasn't the boss said anything to me? Vikram wonders.

"Do you think anyone at CIU could do it?" He doesn't take the name directly but he knows that Vikram is able to understand whom he is hinting at.

After a while, he answers, "Arif is not of that sort. Though he looks cold and rough, he hates criminals to the core. He follows rules to the hilt and won't let anyone else break them either. He is not a schemer, nor someone who could be so easily manipulated, which is the kind you would trust with such a power. So, Arif cannot…"

After a brief silence, he says, "But boss is a complex guy. He is a typical bureaucrat and has to please political bosses. He has to get results to become important in the chain of command. He has the right intentions but he is ambitious as well. So, if you ask me, the boss can get it done."

"Sir, between you and me, the boss is my uncle, but he hasn't been honest with me, either. His real motive to bring me into CIU was to use me to reverse engineer TS-108 secretly, removing the future dependency of its supply from Sudarshan."

Vikram keeps listening. He knows what is coming next.

"Sir, is there anyway, we can test the boss with TS-108?"

"And you have come to me with this request! You know I could just tell the boss and get you fired," Vikram says with a smirk.

"I know that, sir. But from what I have learnt from you, Truth is very important. This unit is bound to fail if it is led by a dishonest boss. If we are mere pawns in a bigger conspiracy, then I am not ready to be a part of it. So, if you get me fired, so be it. I will not be an Abhimanyu to this

Chakravyūha."

The conviction on Suryakant's face says it all. Vikram feels proud looking at his protégé. *His heart is in the right place.*

Vikram considers his options. *If the boss was an interested party in the case, CIU should never have taken this case! He is right. Even if it's a distant possibility, we need to rule it out.*

"I am with you. We need to eliminate this possibility."

"How do we get TS-108, sir?"

The look on Vikram's face is very calm. He opens his drawer and takes out a screwdriver. He gets up from his chair and moves towards a small switchboard in his room behind the fridge. He unscrews the four screws. Then carefully takes out a small test tube. "I think I had saved it for this day."

He hands it over to Suryakant, "Use it wisely."

"Thank you, sir." His instincts about Vikram have been right.

❖❖❖

Chief's Cabin, CIU
November 12, 2 PM

Suryakant knocks on the room. "Sir, I have something to discuss with you regarding the case."

"Yes, come in."

He enters and sits on the chair. He keeps a folder on the table.

"Sir, we have examined the suspects and explored all possible leads. I think it looks like a suicide."

"Are you sure? Have all the leads been explored?" The excitement in his voice is palpable.

Suryakant rubs his forehead with his right hand, pretending to have a headache.

"Do you have a headache?"

"Yes, sir."

"Would you like a cup of tea?" A boss offering a cup of tea is a definite sign that he is pleased with you.

"Wouldn't mind, sir." *He has taken the bait.*

Ajay presses the bell but nobody comes in.

"Sir, the peon probably has gone for lunch. There is nobody outside. I will make it myself."

"Make one for me as well."

Suryakant gets up to prepare some green tea. There is a room separator, so Ajay cannot see what he is doing. Suryakant prepares two cups of tea and adds TS-108 in one of them.

He serves the tea and they both start drinking it.

"What about the death of Shruti?"

"It also appears to be a case of an accident. Very unfortunate turn of events for the family."

"What does the post-mortem report for Sudarshan say?"

"It hasn't come, sir."

He is keeping a close watch on time. "I will take leave, sir." He starts to get up and leave. *When the boss wakes up, he should remember that he had left.*

The TS-108 takes effect and Ajay goes to the unconscious state. Suryakant waits for a while and then quickly calls on intercom number 202 and asks Vikram to come in.

Vikram enters and locks the door from inside. Suryakant starts his interrogation:

What is your name?
Ajay Raj Singh.

Did you kill Sudarshan Chatterjee or Shruti Chatterjee?
No.

Did you have any role in the murder of Sudarshan Chatterjee or Shruti Chatterjee?
No.

Who is the inventor of TS-108?
Sudarshan Chatterjee.

Do you have the diary of Dr. Sudarshan Chatterjee?
No.

Suryakant shakes his head.

Do you have any antidote for TS-108?
No.

Did you tell about Dr. Sudarshan Chatterjee developing the Truth Serum to anyone?
Yes.

Tell the names of those to whom you have told about Dr. Sudarshan Chatterjee being the inventor of TS-108?
Arif Khan and Suryakant Singh.

Why did you tell Arif Khan about Dr. Sudarshan Chatterjee?

I had asked him to keep a watch on Sudarshan. His phone was tapped by him to know what he was up to and to protect him.

Bloody hell. Nothing! Suryakant thinks.

Suryakant whispers to Vikram, "Sir, should I ask about the murder investigation of first wife?"

Vikram says, "No. Some rules should not be broken. We were wrong about him. Keep the teacups back at their place. And let's leave quickly and forget this ever happened."

Suryakant and Vikram leave the room.

Chapter 19
Ichchhā
(The Wish)

SI-3, CIU
November 12, 3:30 PM

He looks at the wall clock in his room. The seconds hand is ticking. He can hear the sound of each tick. Lying on his sofa he is feeling like a desolate sailor with no sight of land. The day has not gone as he had imagined. *Big risk taken for nothing. I felt this was it, but I was so wrong.* Now he actually had a headache and felt the need for a cup of tea.

Suryakant gets a call from Kritika. He picks up.

"Hi."

"You need to come home. Its urgent."

"What happened? Is everything alright?"

"Yes, everything is alright. You need to come here."

"I will be there within an hour."

Residence, Karol Bagh
November 12, 4:30 PM

The door is open. Suryakant enters the room. Kritika and Ayushman are sitting on the sofa. Radhey is in the kitchen. A man in black coat is sitting with them as if some legal proceeding is going on. The atmosphere is tense.

"Kritika, is everything alright?"

"Suryakant sir. This is Advocate Gopal Singhvi. He handles the legal affairs of the company and Baba."

Suryakant goes forward and shakes hand with Gopal Singhvi.

"As police investigation is going on, I needed all three of you to be present before I proceed," Gopal says.

He takes out a sealed envelope. He opens it and takes out the document. "This is the Will of Dr. Sudarshan Chatterjee." He hands a copy of the Will, to each of them. They start to read

I, Dr. Sudarshan Chatterjee, am the absolute owner and in possession of Bungalow at Karol Bagh along with its movable belongings; jewelry kept at Bank of Baroda Karol Bagh branch locker no. 112; 10,000 shares in company SSKA (which is 90% ownership of the company) and the balance in personal bank accounts.

Life is uncertain and after the death of my wife, I do not know when the Almighty might send a call for me, I don't know when I will leave this beautiful world, therefore, during my lifetime I want to make a settlement of all my movable and immovable properties so as to

avoid any differences or dispute over the sharing of my properties among my legal heirs. Therefore, I am making the present will considering the wishes of my wife. So long as I am alive, I will continue to be the owner of all my properties. However, after my death, the above-mentioned properties will be transferred as below:

1. Bungalow at Karol Bagh is to be given to my son Ayushman.

2. The movable belongings in the Bungalow are to be divided equally between my son Ayushman and daughter Kritika.

3. Gold, Diamond and Silver Jewelry kept in locker no. 112 at Bank of Baroda Karol Bagh branch are to be given to Kritika.

4. The shares of the company SSKA are to be transferred to my daughter Kritika alone.

5. Bholeshwar Trust to be dissolved and its assets to be given to its beneficiaries at Bal Shishu Charitable Orphanage as per the Trust deed.

6. The bank balances in all my personal / joint accounts is to be divided equally between my son Ayushman and daughter Kritika.

7. Any other item not already covered above is to be divided between Kritika and Ayushman, in equal ratio.

I bequeath all my movable and immovable properties to my aforesaid legal heirs as per the arrangement made above. I appoint Mr. Gopal Singhvi, s/o Late Sh. Harikant Singhvi, from M/s. Singhvi & Sons, as executor of this Will. All my previous will and testament hereby stand annulled.

Amended and Signed on this 10th November 2025 in the presence of the following witnesses who have also signed in presence of each other and in my presence."

"The last wishes of Late Dr. Sudarshan Chatterjee will be executed as described," Gopal says.

The advocate takes the signature of Kritika and Ayushman. He asks Suryakant to step outside for a moment. Kritika and Ayushman are engaged in reading the Will.

They both step outside the house without anybody noticing them. Gopal hands over a key to Suryakant, and says, "Here is a key to locker no. 108 at SBI bank Karol Bagh Branch which Sudarshan had asked me to secretly hand over to you, in the event of his death."

Suryakant is surprised. Gopal continues, "The day he was released by the police, he came to meet me and gave this key to me. And in the night, he was found dead, probably murdered. Whatever is inside that locker, Sudarshan wanted you to have it."

Locker no. 108. What's with this number and Sudarshan? Suryakant wonders.

Nevertheless, he reluctantly accepts the key to the locker from Gopal and looks at the time. It's close to 5 PM. *The bank will still be open and we can get the locker operated.* He requests Gopal to accompany him to the SBI bank to access it immediately. Without any further delay, they leave for the bank.

SBI branch, Karol Bagh
November 12, 5:30 PM

An anxious Suryakant is standing in front of the locker with the key. *What could be inside? Will I get the answers I have been looking for? Will there be a confession to murder and a suicide note? Or is he going to hand me over the formula for TS-108. But why me of all people. Maybe he didn't trust anyone. But again, why me?!*

The face of Sudarshan in that interrogation room returns to his mind. He takes a deep breath and puts the key in the keyhole. The branch manager, a tall man in his forties, then puts his key in the other keyhole. He rotates the two keys one by one and the locker opens. The branch manager steps aside.

Suryakant looks inside and takes out the contents of the locker. It is a box with a seven-digit password key. There is nothing else in the locker.

The dull looking branch manager asks, "Do you want to keep the box back in the locker or take it away?"

"I am going to take it with me."

"Alright," he locks the locker and hands over one key of the locker to him and moves out.

"Hope you know what to do with it," says Gopal as he leaves the room.

If only I knew the password. He looks at the box for a while. Maybe I can just get it cut open. But there is the danger of breaking or destroying whatever is inside as well. He shakes the box, but there is no sound.

The first thing that comes to his mind is number 108. He types 0 0 0 0 1 0 8 and presses the enter key. Nothing happens. *That would be too easy.* He takes the box away not knowing how to open it. He immediately thinks that 108 in binary system can be written as a seven-digit binary number 1101100. He types 1 1 0 1 1 0 0 and makes another attempt. Again, nothing happens. *If I have to try all one by one, there are 10 million possibilities. That's not an option either.*

He goes out of the bank and sits in his car. He turns it around and looks at the model of the box. It has a Made in Japan logo with Model No. PIF5054SB. He takes out his cell phone and clicks a photo of the box and searches it on google.com. The first search result is a match. *It's the same box as this!* He opens the link and starts reading its features.

"A safe box with 7-digit password key… With each wrong attempt, the waiting period for entering the next attempt doubles." *Wow! That makes it interesting!*

SI-3, CIU
November 12, 7 PM

Suryakant is sitting in his room looking at Sudarshan's file. He is trying to find some connection between the box and Sudarshan. There must be some clue. He starts to look at the photographs of the crime scene. *Maybe I will notice something there.* Even after closely looking at the photos, he finds nothing more than what is already known.

Disappointed, he closes the file and starts to recollect his thoughts. *He chose me for a reason. But why will he not trust his own son or daughter with whatever this is? Does it have something, which might turn out to be dangerous to them and by not giving it to them, he is protecting them. It has got to be something to do with TS-108.*

With his photographic memory, he thinks of some other possible seven-digit numbers from Sudarshan's date of birth, marriage, etc. Four more combinations are tried but they do not work as well. The time gap for next attempt has now increased to 256 seconds.

Distressed, he keeps the box aside and decides to focus on the Will. *The Bungalow to the son but not a single share in the company. Why?*

He calls up Gopal Singhvi.

"Hello."

"Hello, Mr. Singhvi. This is Suryakant."

"Yes, sir, how may I help you?"

"If I remember correctly the Will was made on November 10th. Was it changed or was it freshly created?"

"I cannot say. There is client-lawyer confidentiality."

"But your client is dead and his Will might have to do something with it."

"Still sir, I cannot tell until there is an official notice or a court's order."

Damn it, these lawyers, Suryakant thinks. Before he is about to hang up, Gopal says, "If you read the Will carefully, the answer lies in it."

In a hurry, Suryakant pulls out the copy of the Will and reads it again.

All my previous Will and testament hereby stand annulled... Amended and Signed on this 10th November 2025

This confirms that the Will was changed. This is enough to get an approval for a notice to the lawyer. *What was in the original Will?*

Suryakant rushes to the boss and tells him about the wishes in the Will. He skips the secret part of the Will, the key to a locker.

"Sir, do I have your approval to issue notice to the advocate Gopal Singhvi."

"Yes, go ahead."

He gets the boss to sign the papers.

SI-3, CIU

November 12, 7:30 PM

Suryakant calls up Gopal Singhvi again.

"I have faxed a letter to you."

He pauses and then says, "I need a copy of any earlier Wills of Dr. Sudarshan, if any, at the earliest."

"Yes, sir, I understand. We have received the fax. The documents will be sent via email within 15 minutes."

"Thank you."

Mukesh walks into the room after 20 minutes with the printout of the email received.

"Sir, there are two Wills of Dr. Sudarshan. The first Will was dated June 22, 2025 and second Will was dated November 10, 2025."

"So, the Will was changed right after his release from CIU."

He picks up the earlier Will and starts reading it. In the earlier Will everything was being shared equally between daughter and son. *Earlier the entire shares of the company were divided equally between Kritika and Ayushman, but they are now going solely to Kritika. And as if to compensate for this and bring parity, the bungalow is now going solely to Ayushman.* There is no mention of locker 108 even in the original will. *What is he trying to say?*

If everyone is to be believed, the company was something

which was very close to Sudarshan. Changing the ownership in favor of Kritika, can only mean one thing. Did he fear for his life from Ayushman? Maybe he held Sudarshan responsible for the death of his mother! I think I have my next suspect.

He calls Ajay and tells him about the change in the Will and gets an approval for another TS- 108 test.

I can't tell Kritika about this. She won't understand. My promise is more important.

IR-1, CIU
November 12, 9:30 PM

Suryakant enters the room and gives the bottle of "water" to Ayushman. He grabs and drinks the water at one go.

Arif is anxiously watching from outside the glass window, hoping this time the result will be different.

"It's quite late. What is this about?"

"It's nothing, we just needed your fingerprints and DNA sample for our records."

"But why was I called here so late? The samples could have been collected from college or home."

"We have to ask a few questions as well. This will be over before you know it.

Ayushman goes into the unconscious state and his questioning starts.

```
What is your name?
Ayushman Trivedi

Did you kill Dr. Sudarshan Chatterjee or Shruti
Chatterjee?
```

No.

Did you have any role in the death of Sudarshan
Chatterjee or Shruti Chatterjee?
No.

Do you know anything about Truth Serum or TS-108?
No.

Did you know about the change in the Will of
Sudarshan Chatterjee?
No.

Why does this keep on happening again and again? Suryakant
bangs the table with his hand. He stops the video recorder
and comes out. *Why did I get an unsolvable case as my very first
one?* Suryakant takes out the sheet of paper and strikes off
the last name in the list - *Ayushman.*

Failure seems to have become the new norm in the life
of an otherwise overachiever, Suryakant.

Chapter 20
CHAKRA
(THE CIRCLE)

SI-3, CIU
November 12, 10 PM

Maybe it was just a suicide. I should accept it.
His cell phone phone rings. *Its Kritika. She must have found out about Ayushman being called to the CIU. He must have told her.* With a lot of reluctance and heaviness in his heart, he presses the green button.

"Hi Kritika."

"I didn't expect this from you. You called my own brother to CIU and took his fingerprints and DNA. What are you trying to achieve? To tear my family apart, whatever is left of it?"

"I can explain."

"You did not even call and inform me that my brother is being called to CIU so late in the day. He was all alone and so scared. Maybe all this is just a joke to you and this is just another case for you. But to us, this is our life. I will never forgive you."

"Kri…" Before he could say anything further, she hangs up the phone.

It is over before it could even start. This is what I had feared.

Suryakant looks at the board where he had created the montage. In a slow motion, he moves towards it and begins to dismantle the setup on the board. One by one he removes the photographs.

His eyes stop at the photograph of 'Kritika'. *Why have I not considered her as a suspect till now?*

She has never been carefully considered as a suspect. She is the one who found Sudarshan dead. She is the one who came to me with that conspiracy theory, which has turned out to be all wrong. She didn't seem to be surprised when the Will was read. She tried to misguide me with her suspicion of Deepak Agarwal. Only she knew that her father was working on something important. Maybe Sudarshan told her about TS-108 and that's why she ensured that she got all the shares of the company and Ayushman got nothing in the company. Or maybe she came to know something about the death of her biological mother and held her father responsible. Did she try to get close to me, to avoid her being considered as a suspect? She has been playing me all along…

He takes out the sheet of paper and writes '5. Kritika Chatterjee'.

Two big crimes that one can commit in one's life, not to begin and not to go till the end. He decides to go till the end, even if it means hurting himself.

Chief's Cabin, CIU
November 12, 10:30 PM

"Sir, I want to make one last attempt."

"You are wasting your time Suryakant. It's a suicide. You have questioned everyone with potential motive. All your suspicions have been found misplaced."

"Sir, one person is left."

"Who?"

"Daughter, Kritika Chatterjee."

"The daughter. What motive could she have?"

"If Sudarshan might have told anybody about TS-108, it has to be her. Maybe she has the TS-108 formula. Eventually, she plotted and won her father's trust and got the entire company which could develop TS-108. After taking over the management, God knows what she might do. It is also possible that she came to know about the death of her biological mother and held Sudarshan responsible."

Ajay does not seem convinced.

"Sir, it may be a long shot. But it's the only one left. Let me put her through the test."

"Alright, do it. But let me be very clear. This is the end… The end. After this, you will make the closure report and hand over the case file and I shall not hear a word about this case from you again."

Suryakant agrees. *At least I am getting to test it on the last suspect.*

IR-2, CIU
November 13, 9 AM

Arif and Suryakant are standing looking through the glass window for the same case - a scene they have got used to. Suryakant has a feeling that today is the day when the mystery will be over.

"Should I go and do it?" asks Arif, with a tone which conveyed the delicateness of the situation at hand.

"No, sir. I will do it."

Arif doesn't object to it.

Suryakant enters the room.

"So, calling my brother was not enough! Now you have called me as well. You think I killed Baba? You think I am a monster? Maybe I never got to know the real Suryakant."

Arif is listening. *Something is going on between these two and it seems 'personal'.*

Suryakant gives her the bottle of water to drink, to calm her down. She refuses, "I don't want anything from you."

Does she have some feelings for me? Did she murder her father? Does she know what is in the bottle? His thoughts are now all over the place.

Love is such a primal raw emotion. One realizes that one is in it, just when one is about to get out of it.

Did he even care for me? Was I just a means to solve his case? Does he really think so low of me? Can I even trust him? She is angry but is feeling thirsty as well. After about ten seconds, she picks up the bottle and drinks the water.

He starts to set up the video recorder.

"Why are you setting up the video recorder?"

"This is the procedure we follow here. Whenever a lady is called to CIU, she is videographed."

"The CCTV cameras are already there. They don't work, is it?"

"They work, but they don't record the audio."

I am making a fool out of myself. Calm down, Kritika says to herself.

The effect of TS-108 begins to take place and she goes into an unconscious state. Suryakant takes a look at the glass window and then he presses the start button on the video recorder.

```
What is your name?
Kritika Chatterjee.

What is the name of your mother?
Shruti Trivedi.
```

He is a bit surprised to hear that she treats Shruti Trivedi as her mother. *They were indeed close.*

```
What is the name of your father?
Sudarshan Chatterjee.

Did you kill Dr. Sudarshan Chatterjee or
Shruti Trivedi?
No.

Did you have any role in the death of
Sudarshan Chatterjee or Shruti Trivedi?
No.

Do you know anything about Truth Serum or
TS-108?
```

No.

Did you know about the change in the Will of
Sudarshan Chatterjee?
No.

His instincts have failed him again today but he is more relieved than disappointed. *I was so wrong about her.*

Suryakant leaves the room and meets Arif.

He says, "It's over, sir. One case is an accident and the other is a suicide."

Arif as always has a cold expression. He pushes his hand forward and says, "Congrats. The case is closed."

Arif starts to move out, then turns back, "She seems like a nice girl. The questioning of her brother, put it on me." He smiles and leaves the room. This is the first time he has seen Arif smile.

There are moments in one's life when one desperately wants something that he does not have. But these are the very moments when one should not forget what one already has. Suryakant takes out the sheet from his shirt pocket and strikes-off the name Kritika Chatterjee. All the names are struck-off.

The circle is complete.

PART III

ĀRAMBHA VIRĀM
(END OF THE BEGINNING)

यत्र योगेश्वरः कृष्णो यत्र पार्थो धनुर्धरः ।
तत्र श्रीर्विजयो भूतिध्रुवा नीतिर्मतिर्मम ।।

जहाँ योगेश्वर श्रीकृष्ण हैं और जहाँ धनुर्धारी अर्जुन है ।
वहीं पर श्री, विजय, विभूति और ध्रुव नीति है – ऐसा मेरा मत है।।

Where Krishna is the Master of combinations,
where Partha is the wielder of the bow,
there, I am convinced, would be
glory, victory, growth and firm morality.

[Bhagavad Gita: Chapter 18, Verse 78]

Chapter 21
Duvidhā
(Dilemma)

Human mind is restless. Just like the trunk of an elephant, it needs something to hold on to. Right now, the only thing his mind is holding on to is the box. *Why did he give this to me? What did he want me to know? And why didn't he tell me the password to open it? At least he could have left me a note or message or email of some sort. After all wasn't he going to commit suicide?*

His mind churns these questions, looking for answers, and as if almost in sync, his fingers turn the box looking for one specific answer. It's just a seven-digit password. Suryakant has already made some ten unsuccessful attempts and the time for the next attempt has increased to nearly seventeen minutes.

It is almost the end of the day and he has accepted the suicide theory, but clearly the case is still haunting him. A part of him wanted to discuss the case with Kritika. Just to get a different perspective. One can never see one's own blind spots. But then as always, the rational part reasons with him and he stops. If Sudarshan wanted to involve her, he would not have given the box solely to him. He was a wise man. He didn't want anybody else to know. And then there was an even more fundamental question haunting him - Will she even talk to him?

As his gaze travels the room, he sees the photo of his father sitting poignantly at the top of the corner table. *I wish you were here Papa; life would have been so different. But for you, I do not know if I would have ever returned to India. Destiny brought me here for some purpose. Everything happens for a reason.* His mind comes back to the thought it is clinging on to. The box. *I need to crack this password.*

He tries to remember the discussion he had with Sudarshan.

"Are you a Shiva devotee?"

"Yes."

"We are not very different after all."

The way he said it. 'We both are Shiva devotees.' It has got to do something with Shiva.

He starts visualizing the image of Lord Shiva. Shiva has three eyes (Trinetra), his weapon is a three-forked weapon (Trishul), he is the third one of the Tridev (Brahma, Vishnu and Shiva), he is Trikal Jnani (knower of three times

- the past, present and future) and Trilok Darshi (one who can see the three worlds), three horizontal lines of the ashes can be seen on his forehead and the number of the braids on his hair are three. For this reason, three-pronged Bilva leaf is offered to him, Shiva devotees put three lines on their forehead and three times Pradakshina (circumambulation) is done around lord Shiva`s temple.

Could this be it? Just the number three?

He types 0 0 0 0 0 0 3 and presses the open key. The box still does not open. He will have to wait for nearly thirty-five minutes now.

November 14, 1 AM

If not Kritika, at least Google can give some new perspective. He opens his laptop and searches 'numbers associated with Lord Shiva'. The first link that comes up is 'Why is number 3 associated with Lord Shiva'. He moves to the next one 'Lord Shiva's Favorite Number 8'. He clicks on it and starts to read

Shiva is called Ashta Murthy. Sanskrit word 'Ashta' is the root for English 'eight' and Tamil 'Ettu'.

The Vedas speak of the Ashta Murthys' (forms) of Lord Shiva. Sarva, Bhava, Rudra, Ugra, Bheema, Pasupathi, Mahadeva, Eashana are the eight Murthys of Shiva.

Puranas explain the Adhistanas for these eight forms, which are Sarva for earth, Bhava for water, Rudra for fire, Ugra for wind, Bheema for space, Pasupathi for yajamana, Mahadeva for moon and Eashana for Sun.

A Shiva temple has eight parts. Shivling, Nandi, Platform for offering, Arch behind the god, Curtain or

Maya, Flag staff, Tower representing living being and Sanctum sanctorum equivalent of Mind.

Tamil Nadu boasts of Eight Shrines of Shiva's Eight Heroic deeds known as Ashta Veerattanams.

That's a lot Suryakant does not know about Lord Shiva. His intuition tells him what should be the next number that he should try. The display on the box is back. It is time. He punches in '0 0 0 0 0 0 8'.

The box does not open. He continues his study on the internet. On the Wikipedia page on Lord Shiva, the title 'Five mantras' catches his attention.

Five is a sacred number for Lord Shiva. One of his most important mantras has five syllables (nama śivāya).

Shiva's body is said to consist of five mantras, called the pañcabrahmans. As forms of God, each of these have their own names and distinct iconography:

1. Sadyojāta

2. Vāmadeva

3. Aghora

4. Tatpuruṣa

5. Īsāna

These are represented as the five faces of Shiva and are associated in various texts with the five elements, the five senses, the five organs of perception, and the five organs of action. Doctrinal differences and, possibly, errors in transmission, have resulted in some differences between texts in details of how these five forms are linked with various attributes.

Something tells him that it is unlikely to be the password. The next attempt at opening the box is more than an hour away. It is already late and he is in no mood to wait that long. His eyes are tired and he can barely keep them open. He decides to call it a day.

Hey Bholeshankar show me the way!

November 14, 7:30 AM

Suryakant does not remember falling asleep. All he remembers is seeing Kritika in his dream. It was a pleasant dream, the kind that leaves a smile on your face. *Will Today be the day?* He gets up and goes to brush his teeth.

The door of his bathroom is slightly open. The reflection of the calendar in the bedroom is visible in the mirror above the washbasin. There is an image of Lord Shiva on it. He sees it every day, but today it is as if Bholeshankar is speaking to him. The last words of Sudarshan echo in his mind 'May Lord Shiva show you the way'. 'SHIVA', 'SHIVA', 'SHIVA' the chant fills up his mind. As if in a eureka moment, he spits out the toothpaste and rushes to his study table. Picking up a paper and pen, he begins to place the alphabetical position in name 'Shiva'.

S - 19,

H - 8,

I - 9,

V - 22,

A - 1

Could the number be 1989221. It's a seven-digit number.

He picks up the box, keeps it on his table, punches in 1 9 8 9 2 2 1 and presses the open button. Suddenly, there is a click and the box opens from the top.

The first thing Suryakant notices is that the box has been rigged from the inside to destroy its contents in case of any forced attempt to break it open. There is a thick black silicone casing lining its interior. There are innumerable thin capillaries lining above the silicone on both sides which seemed to be filled with some chemical. A diary sits tightly ensconced in the silicone. *Is this the diary Kritika mentioned?* He carefully pushes his finger, removes it and keeps it on his bed, with extreme caution.

Before opening the diary, out of curiosity, he returns to the table and breaks open one of the capillaries and smells the chemical inside. It is colorless and odorless. He takes out his lighter and tries to burn it, but the fire gets extinguished. With his finger, he takes an infinitesimal pinch of the chemical and places it on the tip of his tongue. It is tasteless. It occurs to him that the chemical must be H_2O, which in common parlance is called 'Water'.

The satisfied engineer in him concludes that the diary must be made of Water-soluble paper. *Genius always lies in Simplicity.*

He reads the engraving on the top of the diary

There are two snakes holding a sword around the title 'NEELKANTH'. He knows that Sudarshan developed the Truth Serum 'TS-108'. *The snake with the sword must symbolize the destruction of crime.*

Wondering why Sudarshan chose him, Suryakant starts seeing the connections between them. '*We both seek to destroy crime,*' the words resonate in his head. '*We both have lost someone close to us,*' he remembers. '*We both hate criminals to the core*'.

There is a surge of adrenaline in his body. The mystery of TS-108 is about to be revealed to him. The baton is about to be passed. The responsibility that comes with it, is making him nervous. His hands are shaking in anticipation.

He opens the diary. On the first page *Om Namah Shivaay* is written in a circular form in Sanskrit language.

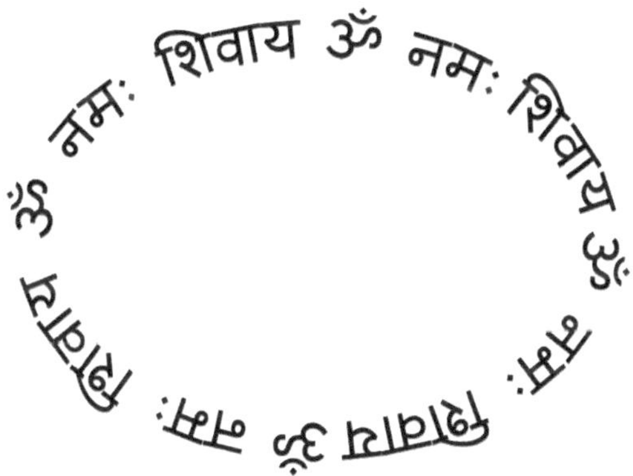

It occurs to him that probably Sudarshan is trying to convey the cyclical nature of everything in the universe through Sanskrit language. *What begins always comes to an end. What ends always has a new beginning.*

The word 'Sanskrit' means well-prepared, pure, refined, or perfect. The language has great logic, precision and elegance making it a powerful language for expression of both scientific and literary thoughts. The alphabets in Sanskrit language are arranged after closely observing the sound of human speech. For instance, the vowels *a, aa, i, ee, u, oo, ae, ai, o, ou* are arranged according to the shape of the mouth when they are emitted - *a* and *aa* are pronounced from throat, *i* and *ee* from palate, *o* and *oo* from the lips, etc. Similarly, for the consonants. It won't be outrageous to say that it is the most scientific language in the world.

Below the cyclic *Om Namah Shivaay*, it is written

> *"Before awakening the Neelkanth,*
> *the shishya must be awakened"*

He doesn't understand much and starts to quickly turn the pages to see what it contains. It's a thick diary. It has many pages of long notes, random drawings, few photographs, and some newspaper clippings. It is unorganized and unconnected. There are a lot of blank pages between the written pages. Based on the location of the blanks, it appears that the diary is divided into three parts. There is no mention of any chemical or the ingredients or the chemical processes to create TS-108. The diary is not what he had expected. His excitement soon fades away.

He goes back to the first page and reads it again. "Before awakening the Neelkanth..." *The secret is encoded in it.*

Sudarshan wants me to read the diary first. He decides to start reading it in the office that day and keeps it in his office bag.

SI-3, CIU

November 14, 10 AM

Suryakant is dressed in his favorite light blue shirt and dark blue pants. His mood is jubilant. The mystery of the box has been solved. With the case closed, there is time to read the diary. He takes out the diary from his bag. It has been barely two minutes when there is a knock on the door. Brijesh enters with a file in his hand. In a flash, he hides the diary in his right drawer and closes it.

"Yes, Brijesh."

"Sir, the post-mortem report has come." Brijesh places it on the table.

"Why was there so much delay in the post-mortem report?"

"Dr. Joshi had not come for the last three days as he was not well. Yesterday, he did the post-mortem and gave the report this morning. He also said he had to wait for some test results before finalizing the report.

Suryakant takes the report and skips right to its end.

Observations:

All clothes were intact, having no cuts or tears. The wrist of the left hand was slit. Left half of the shirt was soaked with blood. The cut in the hand resulted in severe external bleeding. The cut showed that the slit was done slowly and not with a sudden motion.

There were no cuts on any other part of the body, indicating no possibility of any fight prior to death. No other external injuries were present over the body. Internal examination revealed that all organs were pale.

The heart attack was caused due to abnormal presence of clozapine in the blood due to overdose of an antipsychotic drug.

<u>Opinion - Cause of Death:</u>

Stroke/Heart Attack due to abnormal presence of clozapine in the blood.

The last line leaves him in *duvidha*. The death is not due to the cut on the wrist. The actual reason for death is an overdose of an antipsychotic drug. *Why would someone take an antipsychotic drug and then slit his wrist? That's like having plan B in suicide.*

The report is signed by Dr. Ramakant Joshi at the end. He dials on the intercom and asks to speak with Dr. Joshi, just to be sure.

"This is Dr. Joshi speaking."

"Good morning, doctor, this is Suryakant. I was reading your post-mortem report of Dr. Sudarshan Chatterjee. What is your reading for the cause of death?"

"The death is due to heart failure due to abnormal presence of clozapine in the blood."

"That I have read in the report. I wanted to know what you feel - do you think it's a murder or suicide?"

"This being a suicide is very improbable. It is more probable that it was a murder and made to look like a suicide. The glass we found with which the hand was slit appears to be a decoy. We did not find any skin tissue on the glass, but only blood. It looks like the glass was made to *appear* as the murder weapon. The hand was slit with some other object like a knife or something sharp. This time I will give ninety-to-ten chances of murder-to-suicide."

"But you have not mentioned all this in the post-mortem report."

"You were not in the office. So, I discussed with the Chief about the report. He asked me not to put this in the report. He said he had discussed this with you and that you were in agreement."

I am not. "Yes. Thank you, doctor."

God damn it. It is a murder.

But why has Ajay sir withheld this crucial information? It occurs to him that the case is no more a priority for Ajay. When faced with such choices, a practical man generally tends to take the path of least resistance. Clearly Ajay wants him to bury the case, accept it as a suicide and focus on development of TS-108. *What happened to Nānṛtaṃ now?* Suryakant wonders.

An idea suddenly occurs to him. He picks up the intercom and redials the number.

"Dr. Joshi here."

"Doctor, this is Suryakant again. I wanted to know whether this chemical clozapine was found in the blood of Shruti Chatterjee also."

"We normally do not run a test for this chemical…in her case also, we did not, specifically, as death was not due to heart attack, so I will have to run a test to find out."

"Do we have any blood sample to run this test?"

"Yes, we keep some blood samples for six months for any other tests that might be required to be done later."

"Great. Can you please do this test and get back to me at the earliest?"

"I will let you know the result, by this evening."

"Thank you, doctor. And please keep this between us."

With some reluctance, the doctor says, "Ok."

Suryakant hangs up the phone. Brijesh is looking at him with eager eyes.

"What happened, sir?"

"There is one loose end, we need to tie it up or it may open up the Pandora's box again."

"Sir, anything I can do. Where is this box, sir, let me try?"

"No, it's a metaphor." *You stupid.* "Let's wait till the evening. I will let you know."

Brijesh leaves the room. Suryakant's mind just cannot fathom what he will do in case the same chemical is found in the blood of Shruti Chatterjee as well. It cannot be a mere coincidence.

I need to wait for the result.

SI-3, CIU
November 14, 5 PM

The phone rings and breaks the silence of the room.

"Hello."

"Good evening. It's Dr. Ramakant Joshi. The test result has come and it is negative."

"By negative you mean it is not present?" Suryakant tries to re-confirm what he has just heard.

"Yes, that is what negative means."

"Are you sure?"

"Yes," the voice on the other end says in an irritated manner.

Suryakant is disappointed. The spark in his voice is extinguished. But he decides to ask the same question again.

"Doctor, once again, what is your reading – was it an accident or a homicide?"

"She died due a fatal head injury which caused internal bleeding. She was drunk as well. Very difficult to say, it is like fifty-fifty. It may be a homicide or an accident. I think consulting a blood spatter expert or looking at other evidence may be more helpful."

Fifty-fifty chance that it can be murder or an accident. The words resonate in his head. *Is that the way a forensic expert talks?*

"Thank you for your time doctor."

The conservation had ended but the dilemma in his mind remained.

Chapter 22
NIRBALATĀ
(THE WEAKNESS)

Residence, Kirti Nagar
November 14, 11:30 PM

Six cigarette butts are lying scattered on the floor. Suryakant is lying on his sofa and looking outside his window. The pale yellow streetlight is peering inside his room. It's late. On a normal night, Suryakant would have binge-watched cricket or some new sitcom on Netflix. But not today.

He hears a buzz in the room. There is a fly trying to get out through the glass of the closed window but can't see the open door next to it. The fly is hustling hard; it's putting everything in its power. But in the wrong direction.

Don't be that fly, Suryakant thinks to himself.

Mind says that there are no suspects with motive but the heart says there is something more to both the deaths. *But from where should I start even if I want to? All the suspects have been tested on TS-108. There are none left.*

When in doubt, he always looks at his Papa for answers. The photo of Papa is on the table. He closes his eyes and begins to recall what stories his father used to tell him. *Papa tell me something.* He reminisces the time Papa told him the story of 'Blind men and the Elephant'.

It is a story of a group of blind men, who have never come across an elephant before and they learn and conceptualize what an elephant is like by touching it. Each blind man feels a different part of the elephant's body, but only one part, such as the side or the tusk. They then describe the elephant based on their limited knowledge. Each one's description of the elephant is entirely different from the other. This is the *nirbalatā* (weakness) of a blind man. Everyone is telling their truth but not the complete truth.

What I have is the truth as told by each of the suspects and what I have inferred from it. What they have told me is the tail, trunk, legs, tusks of the elephant and not "the" elephant. It is I who need to reconstruct the "elephant" from this.

He calms his mind down and looks around and notices the diary as if it's waiting for him. Addicted to the case and unable to control his urge, Suryakant picks up the diary and starts to frantically flip through the pages.

This is his first moment of solitude with the diary. The pages are not numbered. He starts with the first part.

Atheist (Science) says that a human being is just a biochemical lump that is formed by chance without any governing framework. The entire cosmic manifestation is just a mere coincidence.

Faith (Spiritual) says that the universe is an intelligent design. The biochemical lump has got a mind and a consciousness.

There are some 'why-s' that science can answer but there some 'why-s' which only spirituality can answer. Science answers the relation between mass, speed and energy with equation $E = mc^2$ explaining energy and matter are interchangeable. But why c, the speed of light is a universal constant, and is equal to about 3 lakh kilometers per second is not known, or who has made this rule is not answered. This gap is filled by spiritual thinking.

Scientific and Spiritual thinking need balance and have to work together.

The discussion with Sudarshan on science and spirituality comes to his mind. *He mentioned this to me.*

The next page has a lot of equations and calculations on time, followed by a commentary.

Our scriptures say that the creation is cyclic. The universe and the Earth, along with humans and other creatures, undergo repeated cycles of creation and destruction.

A universe endures for about 4,320,000,000 years (4.32 billion earth years - one day of Brahma, the creator or kalpa) and is then destroyed by fire or water elements. At this point, Brahma rests for one night, just as long as the day. This is called pralaya (cataclysm) and it repeats for 100 Brahma years (313 trillion earth years) that represents Brahma's lifespan.

- Satya Yuga = 1,728,000 Earth years
- Treta Yuga = 1,296,000 Earth years
- Dvapara Yuga = 864,000 Earth years
- Kali Yuga = 432,000 Earth years
- 1 Mahayuga = 4.32 million earth years
- 1 day of Brahma = 1000 Mahayuga
- 1 day of Brahma = 4.32 billion earth years

Science estimates age of Earth to be about 4.54 billion years and life on Earth started about 3.5 billion years ago.

He recalls the calculation. *All the discussion we had on time dilation, meant something.*

Science and Spirituality together is a duality - both are needed - view them together.

He flips to the next page which has thoughts on what life in a cell means. The page has many diagrams followed by discussion.

The creation of cell and life in it is a mystery. We say a cell has life when it is organized (specialized coordinated parts), ability to grow, reproduce and maintain (use energy and consume nutrition to sustain life), homeostasis (dynamic equilibrium) and evolve (ability to adapt with the environment).

A self-sustaining cell has a cyclic life - birth, growth and death just like everything in the Universe.

He takes some time to absorb the thought. *When do we say, something is alive? Never really thought what life actually means.* With this thought, he turns to the next page.

A cell with life turned into complex living creatures which evolved into the human body. The body has an intelligence in the form of mind. A consciousness or atman (soul) ties them. We don't know how!

Body and mind together is a duality - both are interdependent and interconnected for survival of humans.

In the next page he goes ahead and discusses the birth of civilization.

Humans (Purusha) with their imagination and fictions, created and formed societies. These societies started taming nature (Prakriti).

Another duality - both human (Purusha) and nature (Prakriti) need each other. They are also inter-connected. One has no meaning without the other.

This is the end of the first part. The stress on dualism by the guru (teacher) is visible. *By why?* He decides to spend some more time on understanding this dualism and read about it on the internet.

The possibility of murder has made him even more careful. Someone might be looking for the diary. He decides to keep the diary hidden in his room and not take it to the office anymore.

No one should know that I have the diary.

Residence, Kirti Nagar
November 18, 11:30 PM

The last few days, he hasn't been able to spend much time with the diary. Office work has kept him a little occupied. Suryakant is tired but unable to sleep. The first part of the diary has thrown his mind into wilderness, questioning life itself. He gets up and takes a walk around the room. Coming back, he picks up the diary and decides to move to the second part. Most striking feature of the second part of the diary was that it seemed to be grouped into two segments. *Pratyaksh* (Evident) and *Anubhuti* (Realization).

Suryakant feels lost and begins to read randomly

Anubhuti: Human Body is only a vehicle. Mind is the driver. Consciousness is the passenger. That is the real "you".

Interesting insight, Suryakant thinks to himself. *Sudarshan seemed to be influenced by Vedic philosophy.*

Suryakant flips some pages.

Pratyaksh: Physiological process and mental process are two parts of one whole. Whatever we do physiologically affects the mind. Body is the solid state and mind is the ethereal state of the same incipient energy. Alcohol is taken in the body, but it affects the mind. Sexual arousal starts in the mind and then the body responds. But does it affect the consciousness? The real "you"?

Just as the outer petals need to be removed to reach the buds in a flower, Suryakant begins to see the wisdom in Sudarshan's words.

As Suryakant continues to flip the pages, a newspaper clipping falls down. It is an article written by a Hungarian-American psychologist, Mihaly Csikszentmihalyi. Suryakant has difficulty even in mentally pronouncing the name. The article reads, "Our Bandwidth is Limited".

He locates the exact page from where the clip has fallen and continues to read.

> *Pratyaksh: Our supply of attention (otherwise known as "bandwidth") is limited. Mihaly Csikszentmihalyi's research had estimated that we can process about 120 bits per second. This is based on our ability to recognize seven bits of information per attentional unit of time, plus or minus two, and Orme's estimate of our "attentional unit" is 1/18th of a second. In my calculation, this gives humans 18 X 7 or 126 bits per second of processing power. However, our tests with Serum 801 have given us hope that this limit can be increased multiple times. Latest results are showing that the human mind in a state of highest activity under the influence of Serum 801 can process more than 1000 bits per second and shows extremely enhanced synaptic activity. The capacity and speed of mind increases significantly. It is like having Rāvaṇa's ten heads working together.*

Serum is given to the body, but it pushes the limits of the mind, Suryakant continues reading. He is getting more curious about Serum 801.

> *Anubhuti: The human body is impregnated with mysteries, akin to the universe. It is only a difference of scale. What started as a project to enhance human*

capabilities, has given an interesting offshoot. A byproduct. We are naming it Serum 108, a palindromic reference to its properties which are exactly opposite to Serum 801. This serum slows down the synaptic activity considerably and consequently the brain processing speed. This allows the test subject to experience an extremely powerful hallucination. This hallucination is so powerful that the subject does not even recollect having it. Shiva has made me the instrument of his work. These serums together may be the key to achieving the ultimate human pursuit - Excellence.

To really understand something, one needs to understand the reason for its creation. He is mighty impressed by Sudarshan's thought process and continues to read further.

Anubhuti: While administering the serum 108 one should be sure as to who is the real "you", which is responding to the truth serum.

Sensing he has flipped a page too many, Suryakant goes back.

Pratyaksh: Since this posed two edges to the problem, i.e., controlling the mind and controlling the body, I need to tackle this problem in a holistic way, a two fronted attack. Control the mind as well as the body. Only when this science is perfected, will the serum 108 "really" work.

Suryakant is amazed. He had thought about TS - 108 merely as a chemical which switched off some part of the brain. It was much more than that!

Pratyaksh: It is only logical to start with the body, because the body is the portal to the mind. If you control the body, you can with a high degree of certainty, control the mind.

As he reads, the next page, Suryakant's eyes widen.

Anubhuti: Body controls the mind and vice versa. When one gets angry, one's breathing rhythm disrupts and breathing becomes faster. But vipassana has shown that by controlling one's breathing, one can control one's anger. Similar results are seen when the truth serum is administered, the breathing slows down. As the breathing slows, so does the mind. If one is masterful and can bring back the breathing to the normal rhythm, then his mind will continue to remain alert and in complete control despite the administration of the truth serum. We need to do further research to perfect this serum.

TS-108 is not infallible and it has flaws. *Someone has indeed gamed the system. I just need to figure out who!* Suryakant says to himself as he dozes off to sleep.

Chapter 23
Khoj
(Search Continues)

SI-3, CIU
November 28, 5:15 PM

Nearly two weeks have elapsed. Normalcy has returned to CIU. Suryakant had to abruptly go to Mumbai for a rather long training on Digital Forensics for five days. Due to this, even the boss did not assign any independent case to Suryakant but had him work with Vikram on one case, which was cracked with precision as usual. He hasn't met or talked with Kritika. Nor has he been able to spend time with Sudarshan's diary. But, going by whatever he had read, his admiration for Sudarshan and his work had only grown by leaps and bounds. More than anything, it has been a journey of learning and introspection for Suryakant.

He, however, has not been able to make any further breakthrough in the case. His gut says that, at least Sudarshan was murdered, if not Shruti. His recent rendezvous with Sudarshan's diary has emboldened his theory further. *I am unable to find the murderer, as either the murderer knew how to cheat the TS or the murderer has not been considered as a suspect. But how? There are no perfect crimes. Every criminal, no matter how smart, always leaves a trail of breadcrumbs. Where are my breadcrumbs?*

Troubled, he diverts his mind and picks up the day's newspaper and starts to read. He loves cricket. The Champions Trophy tournament is going on. In yesterday's match, Shourya has hit 32 runs in the last over to win the match. 6-6-4-6-4-6 was the scorecard in the last over. This is the highest anybody has managed to score in the last over and win a match for the chasing side. *Are these matches scripted? They seem too good to be true! Just like this case.* He realizes his mind has again connected it to the case. Shaking his head, he turns the pages of the newspaper looking for some other story. One piece of news catches his attention.

Another PhD student commits suicide - student body raises the issue of undue pressure

He knows the pressure on research scholars. It was one of the reasons he didn't go for a PhD. He starts to read further,

When Naveen Mehta's wife couldn't get him on the phone for one entire day, she informed others in the PhD scholar's hostel of a reputed college here at Delhi. He was found dead in his room with his left wrist cut by glass.

Naveen Mehta, 32, was from Bihar. He joined the PhD

program in 2019, and was working to earn a PhD in chemistry for the last six years.

He was under tremendous pressure for completion of his PhD thesis, his family and close friends have informed. Also, he was recently married and his research work was affecting his married life as well, his friends have informed the police.

This is the second such incident in the college. Another PhD student from Tamil Nadu, Sharath V, took his own life last year. The students' body has raised the issue that undue pressure is being put on scholars to complete their thesis within five years. A recent study has shown that 1 in 3 PhD students consider suicide.

However, the police officials are tight lipped about the case and have stated that further investigations are in progress.

One in three. That's a very high rate. Is it real, or another made up statistic by the media?

He again starts to read the news and notices: *He was found dead in his room with his left wrist slit by glass. Sudarshan's left wrist was also slit.* His mind has again taken him back to the case.

Suryakant tries to focus on some other news but news of a young scholar just like him, committing suicide makes him curious to know more about him. He decides to login on DPoCS - Delhi Police Crime database Server. Access to the server is one of the privileges of being in CIU. Searching by the name of the victim Naveen Mehta and the date of crime in the last three days, yields one result. He opens the case file and clicks on the photos of the crime scene. Seeing the photos, he feels sad for the newly married couple. The post-mortem report is available and he starts reading it. As he reads the report, his heart rate starts to rise rapidly. He feels his heart pound as his eyes gaze on the last line of the report.

<u>Opinion - Cause of Death:</u>

Stroke/Heart Attack due to abnormal presence of clozapine in the blood.

This was an uncanny resemblance to Sudarshan's death! He goes through the entire post-mortem report. It was as if he was reading Sudarshan's post-mortem report again.

This is impossible. Could there be a serial killer? Suryakant takes out a paper and begins to write.

What are the facts?

Two deaths - husband and wife - both in a very suspicious manner - one made to look like a suicide and the other made to look like an accident.

Suspects considered - Deepak Agarwal, Indu Mehra, Ajay sir, Ayushman, Kritika

Not considered as suspects - Satish Kapoor, Priya Mehta, Gopal Singhvi, Arif, ...

Could it be some Serial killer???

He keeps the pen down and wonders why would a serial killer murder two from the same family, knowing fully well that a police investigation is going on and the chances of getting caught are high. The time window from Sudarshan's release from CIU to his death is also very small.

Can it be about the diary? I need to be extra careful. The image of Bholeshankar he saw before opening the box flashes before his eyes. To Suryakant, it almost feels as if an act of God or a divine inspiration is asking him *not* to give up on the investigation yet. Now that a serial killer has become a possibility, he decides to explore it.

Suryakant takes out the two files marked as 'Case No. 27' and 'Case No. 28'. They are stamped as 'Closed' on their cover. He himself had stamped them such. There is a thought about telling the boss that he wants to re-open the cases based on a wild hunch. But Suryakant knows that Ajay is quite satisfied with the accident and suicide theory and he won't like the cases to be reopened. Can't tell him right now. He strikes-off 'Closed' and starts going through the files again to find something he might have missed.

He opens the files and starts going through them. When he reaches the section that contains the call records, he remembers Vikram sir had said that CDR doesn't lie and it tells you more than the actual person ever will. Suryakant is hoping that it might give some new lead. *I don't have the call record of Ajay sir. Should I get them? But won't that require a clearance from the higher ups? Improbable that I will be able to get it.*

Suryakant goes to the call record of Shruti and starts going through the maximum call duration list. From the same, it occurs to him that she used to talk very frequently with a doctor, a fact which did not seem relevant earlier.

He immediately calls Mukesh on the intercom, "I need the details of the person to whom cell phone number 61934 83483 belongs."

"Right, sir."

"How much time will this take?"

"3 to 4 hours."

"Again, so much time? I am not asking for the call records."

"Sir, getting the KYC (Know Your Customer) details takes the same amount of time as call records."

"Ok."

He hangs up and continues to go through the case files looking for some more clues in the photographs and statements. After twenty minutes, he seems to be going nowhere.

SI-3, CIU
November 28, 8 PM

An idea sprouts in Suryakant's head. It occurs to him that the quickest way to establish a connection will be to get the phone record of this PhD victim, Naveen Mehta, and see if there is any common person between the three death victims.

Suddenly, there is a knock on the door. *It must be Mukesh, I didn't expect him to come so fast.*

Mukesh enters and gives him the KYC documents.

"You got the details quite fast."

Hiding the fact that he made personal efforts to get the details quickly this time, Mukesh says, "Lucky, sir."

Suryakant picks up the KYC pages and looks at the photograph of the doctor.

Mukesh continues, "The doctor is Kiran Malhotra, she is a psychiatrist. She is 42 years old and has an office cum residence at Sector - 42, Janakpuri. I have verified it on the internet."

It's a lady. So, we can rule out any love angle.

"The office address is in the KYC documents. Sir, can I leave? I have to go to a gathering."

Since morning, Suryakant has heard two other colleagues mention about a party. *Am I the only one not invited?*

"Is there a party?"

"No, sir, just a get-together of five or six close families. We stay in the same housing complex."

He realizes that there is indeed a party, but he is not invited. "Ok. You can go. But I need CDR for this number as well." He picks up a page and starts writing Naveen's cell phone number looking at the DPoCS software on computer screen and hands it over to Mukesh.

"Send the request so that we have it first thing in the morning."

"Ok, sir." Mukesh leaves feeling relieved.

I should also get going. He picks up the phone and notices a message from Kritika. He has missed it in the excitement of going through post-mortem reports. Feeling regretful for having missed it, he immediately opens the message and reads it.

"Hi, if you are free, we can meet for dinner at Angithi, CP? Kritika." The message was sent at 7:22 PM.

His happiness knows no bounds. He checks the time and realizes it's 8:25 PM. *Oh, God!* He immediately calls Kritika.

"Hi."

"Hi there. Sorry I saw your message just now. Hope I am not too late."

"I thought you might be too busy to reply."

"Not very busy. Just doing some paperwork. If you are still available for dinner, we can meet."

"Yes, let's meet in 20 minutes."

"Ok. See you soon."

Suryakant hangs up the phone. *It seems her anger had subsided. She must have realized that I was just doing my duty. Finally, the day ends on a good note.* He keeps everything in the drawer, locks it and quickly leaves the office. As he comes out of his cabin, he realizes that the office is empty. He is the last one to leave. Everyone must have gone to the party.

I am going for a date too, Suryakant smiles and leaves.

Angithi Restaurant, Connaught Place
November 28, 9 PM

"Hi."

"Hi, how are you doing? Joined office?"

"Not yet. Don't feel like going to the office so soon. I am thinking of quitting the job and joining the company. I need to carry forward Baba's legacy. Any progress in the investigation?"

"Working on something. But it is a long shot."

She gets curious and her eyes light up. "What are you working on?"

"It's too premature to tell you anything. Will tell you if it leads anywhere."

"I miss them so much."

"I can understand. I too lost my father few years back and it changed me. Change is hard, but it makes you strong. Sometimes it makes you do what you really wanted to do. I believe in destiny and everyone has to achieve his or her own. We all have our small parts to play in God's large design."

Listening to him talk this way, makes her feel as if Baba is talking to her through him. Kritika too is beginning to sense a stronger and deeper connection with him. The talk is interrupted by a waiter who has come to take their order.

"May I take your order, sir?" handing over the menu card, "Would you like to start with some soup or starters?"

Suryakant looks at Kritika. This is the first time they are out together to a restaurant.

"No, we will go directly to the main course. We are quite hungry," Kritika answers.

"Right, Ma'am. The main course menu starts from the fifth page."

Turning over the page, Kritika asks Suryakant, "What would you like to have?"

"Anything except mushrooms," he answers.

They turn over and place the order. Suryakant readily agrees to whatever Kritika suggests. The waiter leaves. Finally, they start talking again.

"I still don't believe that Baba can commit suicide. He wouldn't leave us alone. I don't know anything about the company or how to run it."

"Why do you think he gave you the full control of the company and nothing to your brother?"

"I don't know. He must have had his reasons. Anyways, Ayush is too young to look after the company, so Baba left him the house and the company to me."

"How is Ayushman doing?"

"Ayush has always been a calm and composed boy. But

recently even he has been frequently losing his temper over trivial things. Tragedy this big can break anyone. Why did this happen to our family, we were so happy together!"

"Why did Rama have to leave for vanvas when everything seemed so perfect? It is destiny, life is not fair and will not be fair. Everything may change in the blink of an eye. Never forget you and your brother are still alive and have to carry on your father's legacy."

"Did he say anything about us to you?"

"Not really, but he has left a lasting impression on me, even though we met for a very brief period of time. He wanted me to do something, which even I am trying to figure out."

She gets curious. "What do you mean?"

Realizing that he has said more than he should have, "I mean we shared our thoughts briefly on life and stuff. He said some things to me as well, to guide me. I am sure he would have spoken to you as well and wanted you to carry on with the company. He probably felt you will steer the company out of the crisis it is facing, in the best possible manner."

She starts thinking about what her Baba had told her. There is silence for some time before the waiter interrupts yet again and serves them their order. Since they both were quite hungry, they don't mind the interruption. The hungrier you are, the more delicious the food tastes. The rest of the evening is spent in discussing about each other's past. She is surprised to know that Suryakant was a pharmacist before he turned his sights on service to the nation, which is more stressful, less paying, but definitely more rewarding. They both seemed to be enjoying each other's company.

As they come out of the restaurant, he offers to drive her home. This time she agrees. The drive is short but is the most enjoyable drive Suryakant has ever had in his life.

Residence, Karol Bagh
November 28, 11 PM

She gets out of the car. He also gets down from the other side. She smiles and says, "Good night."

"Good night."

As she moves away towards the gate, he says, "Kritika, please call me if you ever need anyone to talk to."

"Thanks for everything. Please call me Kriti." She smiles and waves goodbye to him. It's a smile that reveals a lot.

On the way home and for the rest of the night, he does not think about the case or its mystery or even the diary. He feels his khoj (search) for someone is over.

Chapter 24
RĀKSHASA
(THE DEVIL)

SI-3, CIU
November 29, 9:30 AM

The trouble with being punctual is that there is no one to appreciate it. The office bears a deserted look. He realizes it's a Saturday and the staff must have partied hard the previous night. He goes and sits in his room.

After about an hour, Mukesh enters, "Sir, I got the call record for the number you wanted yesterday. The soft copy is in your email, sir."

"Thanks, Mukesh. How was the party, I mean the get-together, yesterday? Did you all have a good time?" he asks with a smile.

"It was good, sir." Mukesh smiles back. *Was that sarcasm or is sir in a good mood today?* he thinks to himself.

"Anything else, sir."

"I will call you in case I need anything. Thanks. Please ask the peon to send in a coffee."

"Right, sir," he leaves.

Suryakant puts call records of all the suspects along with the new victim's in the CDR analysis software. He uses Naveen's CDR as a reference and then clicks on the 'Search Common' button to see if there is any common number between the new victim and the two old ones along with all the suspects. He waits for the result.

"No common number found."

Suryakant is disappointed again. He had expected to find the killer at the click of a button. That does not happen.

He picks up the intercom and calls Brijesh. "I need the full case file for case number 1428 of 2025 in the name of Naveen Mehta at Dwarka Police station."

"Yes, sir. I will have to go and get it from the police station. I will get it by the evening."

"Get going then."

He hangs up the phone.

Suryakant remembers the lecture at NPA on Crime Investigation. The speaker had said

The most important rule for a good investigator is to explore all possible leads. Crime is like a jigsaw puzzle and all the pieces should fit together. There is an explanation for everything that has happened. Most cases might get solved by hunches and leads that may look like dead ends.

With nothing much to do, he decides that visiting Dr. Kiran Malhotra might be a worthwhile exercise. If nothing, he may get some personal information about Shruti from her. Maybe Mrs. Chatterjee was consulting her regarding marriage or an affair or something else.

Dr. Malhotra's Clinic, Janakpuri
November 29, 11:30 AM

Suryakant notices the board Dr. Malhotra Clinic on the first floor of the building. He quickly climbs the stairs and presses the bell on the door. It is an office cum residence.

A middle-aged lady comes and opens the door.

Suryakant shows his police ID and says, "I am here to see Dr. Malhotra on a case I am investigating." The lady gets a bit scared but asks him to come inside and be seated.

Suryakant sits on the single-seater sofa in the drawing room. Each item in the room looks like an antique piece, carefully selected and placed. He looks around the room, and notices that there are no family photographs. *That's odd.*

"She is with a patient. I will let her know that a police officer is here."

She goes rushing in. Within a minute, another lady dressed in a blue saree walks out. The lady is around 45 years old and looks much more composed and relaxed. The glasses on her face are striking. She comes and sits on the sofa opposite to him.

"Hello, officer."

The confidence in her voice tells him this is not the first time she is meeting a police officer. "My name is Suryakant Singh. You are Dr. Malhotra, a psychiatrist, right?"

"Yes."

"Since how long you have been practicing?"

"Nearly, fifteen years now."

"Do you live alone here?"

"Yes. But why are you asking me these kinds of questions?"

"I am sorry, let me explain. I am working on the death of Mrs. Shruti Chatterjee. If I am not wrong, she was a patient of yours."

"I am not at liberty to discuss my patients. Their names, problems or discussions are strictly under patient-doctor confidentiality."

"You know we are investigating her murder."

"I know officer, but my job requires me to protect my patients at all cost. I cannot discuss anything further until you get a court order, which decrees that access to the patient case history is relevant to your investigation."

The reply leaves him blank. Suryakant realizes he is not going to get anything further out of her. *She is a cold-hearted devil.*

He quietly leaves.

SI-3, CIU
November 29, 1 PM

Suryakant enters his office in frustration. *These doctors and their doctor-patient confidentiality. My ass!*

He calls Mukesh to his room. *I should have called for her call records yesterday itself along with the KYC details.*

Mukesh enters the room and waits for instructions.

"I want call records for this number."

Mukesh nods and leaves.

He gets back to the case at hand assuming there is a killer somewhere. *I know it.* After nearly one hour of pondering, he keeps the files down and looks at the clock. It is already two o'clock. He is feeling hungry. He picks up the phone to see if there is any call or a message from Kritika. He is hoping for a lunch call from Kritika, but there is no message or call from her till now. He gets up to eat the lunch his mother packs for him every day.

SI-3, CIU
November 29, 3:30 PM

Brijesh and Mukesh enter the room together. "Sir, got the call record for the doctor. It is in the email." Mukesh goes first. Brijesh goes next, "Sir, got the case file for case no. 1428 of 2025 as well."

Suryakant gets up and starts with the case file. High hopes are riding on this hunch. He first reads the profile of the victim and then quickly moves to the report of the investigating officer.

Victim was 32 years old and working towards a Ph.D. His research was not going well and he was under pressure. Further, he was married just 6 months back to a girl of his parent's liking, much against his wishes. He continued to meet his girlfriend even after his marriage.

As per the autopsy report, he died of a heart attack. He probably was in depression and therefore killed himself with an overdose of sleeping pills and then slit his left wrist. Both his wife and his girlfriend were not in the city at the time of death. No evidence of any foul play was noticed.

It is therefore concluded that the cause of death was suicide triggered by multiple personal reasons.

To Suryakant it seems that this boy had read about Sudarshan's suicide in the newspaper and then committed suicide in a similar manner! The investigation report sounds logical and it appears to be another dead end.

Dejected, Suryakant sits down in his chair. Brijesh and Mukesh have no clue what is happening. "What happened, sir?" Mukesh tries to gauge the situation. Suryakant realizes that they both are still in the room.

"Nothing."

Mukesh's presence reminds Suryakant about the doctor. He slowly opens the phone record of the doctor and adds it to the CDR analysis software. The call records of all other victims are already loaded in the software. As a last-ditch effort, he uses Dr. Kiran's CDR as a reference and then clicks on the 'Search Common' button to query for any common call matches. Only this time the screen reads,

"1 common number found."

He clicks on the prompted box. The number appears on the screen and it leaves him in shock.

Suryakant rushes to pick up the case file no. 1428 of 2025 and starts to read it again in haste, looking for something. After turning a few pages, he finds the connection. He feels more sad than excited.

Could this be it? Have I just found the Devil?

Dr. Malhotra's Clinic, Janakpuri
November 29, 8 PM

Suryakant along with Mukesh and Brijesh are standing in front of the building where Dr. Kiran Malhotra lives. He needs the patient file and her notes from the office. It is unlikely she is going to hand them over, even if he requests again. There is only one way now. It needs to be stolen from her office. Her residence and office are the same. Thankfully, she lives alone. He just has to find a way to get her out of the house.

Suryakant is not a criminal, not even the born police-officer type. He is not good at breaking the law.

What would Vikram sir do? he thinks.

At once, the next step becomes clear. Mukesh is asked to stay in the car with clear instructions. Along with Brijesh, he moves two buildings away.

He has decided to do the simplest of things to get her out of the house. All set, he makes the call. Kiran is preparing dinner when she hears the phone ring. She switches off the gas stove and goes to pick up the phone.

"Hello, who is speaking?"

"Dr. Malhotra, this is police officer Suryakant Singh. I met you in the morning."

She immediately recognizes the voice. "Yes, officer. How may I help you now?"

"There is something I want you to see and offer your advice as a psychiatrist. This time it is your expert opinion that I am seeking, not access to your records. I respect your reasons for not sharing the patient's case records, earlier in the day."

"My opinion? What do want me to see?" a confused Kiran asks.

"Can you please come over to the CIU office? I know it is late but had the matter not been very urgent, I would not have disturbed you. I have already sent a vehicle to your home. My inspector Mukesh will escort you to my office. He must be reaching your building shortly."

She goes and peeps out from the window. A police van is already standing outside the building gate. It must be something very important. It is not every day that one is asked to give advice to the police. "Alright, give me ten minutes to get ready."

Suryakant is elated with the reply. "Thanks a lot doctor. Your advice as a consultant will be crucial." The ploy has worked.

After nearly ten minutes, Dr. Kiran Malhotra walks down and sits in the police van. Mukesh has been instructed to take her through the most congested route and only after he gives a green signal, Dr. Kiran can be brought in to CIU. As soon the van leaves, Suryakant tells Brijesh to keep a taxi ready and instructs him to not let anyone come up. He then enters the building. As he had already visited the house in the morning, he already knows that there are no CCTV cameras in the building and outside the house. Even otherwise, he has exercised precaution and has covered his face. He may not be a criminal, but thanks to CIU and Vikram sir, he has learned to break some basic locks like the one at her door. He thinks one more time about what he is about to do. *Even Lord Krishna had to bend some rules to win the war. In the larger scheme of things, breaking the law is CIU's USP anyways and this seems a much smaller crime.* He goes ahead and begins to pick the lock. *Oh Lord! Let there be are no alarms.*

The lock opens and no alarm goes off. Suryakant is relieved. He has a rough idea of the layout of the house. The first room he walks into, is the office. There is a steel cupboard with four shelves. There is no lock on it. The case records are arranged in alphabetical order. He moves to the right alphabet and finds the case file he is looking for. In haste, he starts clicking photographs with his cell phone. In the next five minutes, he finishes the scanning the file and puts it back in its place. Without wasting any time, he leaves the house feeling elated as if he has pulled off a major bank heist.

The whole exercise has been completed with absolute precision in ten minutes. Brijesh is waiting for him in a taxi, ready to leave. He quickly hops in it and tells the driver to take him to the office. In the car, he starts to read the scans on his cell phone. *Childhood trauma…violent tendencies…medical prescriptions…everything fine for many years but since the last month, things are not normal…This could be the key if my hypothesis is right.* The office is barely five minutes away. He leaves a message on WhatsApp to Brijesh with a thumb's up emoji. This is the green signal.

He reaches the office. After fifteen minutes, Dr. Kiran reaches the office.

SI-3, CIU

November 29, 9 PM

Mukesh takes her directly to Suryakant's office. After fifteen minutes of discussion, she comes out and Mukesh proceeds to drop her home.

Suryakant sits in his chair in shock. In the words

of Sherlock Holmes - once you eliminate the impossible, whatever remains, no matter how improbable, must be the truth. He has got the answers that no one was hoping to find. *This is the reason you gave the diary to me.*

With a heavy heart, he picks up the phone and tells Brijesh to bring her in.

Chapter 25
CHAKRAVYŪHA
(THE TRAP)

IR-2, CIU
November 29, 10:30 PM

The Interrogation room bears a somber look. The suspect is sitting on the interrogation chair. The room is dimly lit. The microphone has been silenced and the live CCTV footage is still not being relayed to the outside area of the IR-2. Four pairs of inquisitive eyes are looking at the suspect from behind the opaque glass of the interrogation room. None of them can make out who the person is. All look puzzled. The entire sequence of events has unfolded very fast in the last one hour and Suryakant has been tight lipped about it to all of them. Constable Varsha was given only one terse instruction by Suryakant. *Get them assembled in IR-2 by 10:15 PM*

Fidgeting with her phone, Varsha is the first one to walk

inside the interrogation room. She is carrying a file which contains some background information about the suspect and a small black case. She places the file and the case on the table, before the suspect, a common intimidating technique used in interrogation. *The fear of the ensuing unknown.*

Suryakant is the next to walk in. He is carrying a bottle of water; his new normal in the interrogation process. He sits next to Varsha. Not just next to her, but uncomfortably close. He switches on the microphone and the CCTV. The lights are now turned on. The cast of the room are now on full display to the four confused audience outside the IR -2.

"So, Varsha, how was the party yesterday?"

"Sir, it was good. We missed you there."

"Ah, Varsha. This case. Anyways we avoid being seen together in public right? How about your place tonight?"

"Tonight, sir?"

"Ya. We should get free within the next hour."

"Sir, today my husband Sanjay will be at home."

"Oh c'mon, we have had our little sojourns earlier also! Let's take a small detour on the way home tonight as well."

"I hope our small affair is not getting serious."

Suryakant glances at the suspect and then bends towards Varsha. He goes closer to her, holds her hand and whispers something naughtily into her ear. Varsha blushes and leaves the room. The suspect squirms uncontrollably in the chair with eyes closed. The suspect's face steadily turns red with rage. Suryakant can see the suspect's fists getting clenched and legs shaking heavily.

It has all been played out in his head multiple times. Like a shrewd leopard hiding behind a bush, waiting for his prey, Suryakant waits for his moment. The suspect's eyes close. Suryakant waits. Suddenly, the suspect bangs a fist on the table, very hard. The impact is so strong that it renders a dent on the table. Suryakant asks the suspect, "What is your name?"

The suspect rolls his eyes vehemently, as if in a trance. Suryakant asks again, "What is your name?"

"RUDRANSH." *Part of Rudra.* He screams and opens his eyes.

Suryakant knows this is the moment. The suspect is not going to drink the water. But he has come prepared for this. He takes out the TS-108 from the case which Varsha had left behind and injects it in the arm of the suspect in a flash. Suryakant can see the anger in the eyes of one of his audiences.

The TS-108 takes effect and it begins,

What is your name?
Rudransh.

What is the name of your father?
Rudra Trivedi.

What is the name of your mother?
Shruti Trivedi.

Do you know Ayushman?
Yes. He is a loser. He is weak. He cannot see the Adharma. He does not act against the adulterers, the pāpīs. So, I must intervene to deliver cosmic justice and restore Dharma.

Do you know Dr. Sudarshan Chatterjee?
Yes.

Did you kill Shruti Trivedi?
No.

Did you kill Dr. Sudarshan Chatterjee?
Yes.

Why did you kill Dr. Sudarshan Chatterjee?
He was an adulterer, a pāpī. He was having an affair with Indu. He cheated on my mother and then killed her.

Did you see him killing your mother?
No. But I know what I heard.

What is it that you heard?
I heard him say that he had confessed but the police let him go.

Suryakant is taken aback. The reply pierces his heart. But he continues. Time is running.

How did you kill Dr. Sudarshan Chatterjee?
I gave him a heavy dose of my Iozapin tablet. After he fainted, I slit his wrist with a knife.

Did you kill Naveen Mehta?
Yes.

Why did you kill Naveen Mehta?
He was an adulterer, a pāpī. He was also cheating on his wife.

How did you kill Naveen Mehta?
I gave him a heavy dose of my Iozapin tablet. After he fainted, I slit his wrist with a

knife.

Was the same knife used to murder both Naveen
Mehta and Sudarshan Chatterjee?
Yes.

Where is the knife?
It is kept in the toolbox of my bike.

Have you killed anyone else?
No. But Varsha is next.

IR -2, CIU
November 29, 10:45 PM

Suryakant comes out of the interrogation room to the observation room. Kritika, Ajay, Vikram, and Arif are standing. Ayushman is sitting on the chair, in IR – 2 exhausted. Ajay, Vikram and Arif step forward. They congratulate him.

Ajay goes first, "Well done, Suryakant."

"It would not have been possible without you, sir."

They leave the room. Only Suryakant and Kritika are left. Kritika is in tears. In her heart she knows what is going to happen next as they both also leave the room.

SI-3, CIU
November 29, 11:15 PM

Suryakant looks at Kritika and says, "I have a lot to explain. You remember I told you about a long shot I was working on."

"Yes."

"In the autopsy of your father, we found the presence of the chemical clozapine in his blood. This suggested that his death was due to an overdose of an antipsychotic drug. The glass found in the other hand which we thought was used to slit the wrist was actually a decoy. It indicated that he was possibly murdered but the entire incident was made to look like a suicide."

Tears roll down from her eyes on recollection of that fateful night.

"Your father was working on something very important. What I am about to tell you cannot leave this room."

She nods. "I understand."

"He had created a chemical called TS-108 which when consumed takes complete control of person, both his body and his mind. Then whatever is asked, the person is compelled to tell the truth. It is as if his hand is on The Gita for some time. Whatever he tells is nothing but the truth. We had run this test earlier on your father, Deepak Agarwal, Indu Mehra, Ajay Raj sir, Ayushman and on you as well."

Kritika gets shocked on hearing this. "But I don't remember any such test being done on me."

"That is the specialty of this chemical. It takes complete control of the body and mind and when its effect wears out, the person has no recollection of this test having been done. The test seemed to have worked perfectly until this case came along. In this case, none of the persons we tested accepted any role in the death of your father or your mother. We had also closed the case but then we found one more case which also had been accepted as a suicide but had an uncanny resemblance to the death of your father."

"Who was he?"

"He was Naveen Mehta, a Ph. D student at NSIT, Delhi. He stays in the same hostel as your brother."

Kritika keeps listening without saying anything.

"We further found that your mother had been talking very frequently with a psychiatrist, Dr. Kiran Malhotra. Do you know her?"

"No."

"Initially, we thought maybe your mother was seeing her for some personal problem. But when we matched her call records, we found she had made frequent calls to one more person."

The expression on Kritika's face gets tense and she knows where this is going.

"Your brother Ayushman was undergoing psychiatric treatment under her. Did you know about it?"

"No. No one ever told me anything about this. But I had noticed some medicines he used to take."

"Only your father, mother and Ayushman knew about it. We checked his case history with the psychiatrist. He had a very unfortunate childhood. He had witnessed the death of his biological father, Rudra Trivedi who was caught cheating on his mother. Ashamed, under the weight of his guilt, he committed suicide in front of your brother who was just 4 years old then. Rudra probably said something to him before suicide. This left a lasting impression on his mind. From the case history with his psychiatrist, I learnt that he had violent urges whenever he heard about someone cheating on his or her partner. He had, what is called in common parlance, a *split personality disorder.* His other self Rudransh takes over and compels him to murder any person who commits adultery, an *adharma* in his eyes."

"But you yourself said that he was put through that truth test earlier and he did not confess to murdering anyone?"

"I know. Even I was bothered by this fact to no end."

Kritika listens intently.

"Your father was a genius who had his heart in the right place. He created this serum for the benefit of mankind. Its sole purpose was to remove criminals from the face of this planet. But his work was not perfected. TS had some limitations. He had discovered that a person suffering from split personality disorder is not even aware of the other personality. What the other personality does, is not known to the real personality. The real personality doesn't even know or remember about any action committed by the other personality. So, when TS test is done, only the personality, which is active at that time, answers to the questions. When we first questioned your brother, his real self - Ayushman answered, who was not aware of any murder. This is the flaw of the TS test which we have come to realize now. But your father probably knew this flaw."

Kritika starts to cry. "But Mumma and Baba never told me any such thing. They never even told me about this problem with Ayushman."

"Something happened last month which changed him. Dr. Kiran told me that Ayushman was under medication and things were under control but something happened in the last month which changed him."

"You are saying 'something' happened. What happened in the last one month?"

"That even I don't know. This is one piece of the puzzle which I am yet to find. Maybe he stopped taking his medications and instead used them to commit murder."

Kritika recollects the change in Ayushman's behavior since the last one month. He had suddenly become short-tempered.

"I had to set-up a *chakravyūha* (trap) to uncover this mystery. I asked Varsha to fake an extra-marital affair with me in front of Ayushman to bring out Rudransh. Then I injected him with TS-108 and the truth was revealed."

Kritika closes her eyes. "The rest, well…you have heard." He hugs her.

Chapter 26
Ardha-Satya
(Half-Truth)

SI-3, CIU
November 30, 11 AM

The murder weapon has been found. Forensics confirmed the presence of fingerprints of Ayushman and blood of Sudarshan and Naveen on it. Ayushman is placed under arrest.

Suryakant had a brief talk with Ayushman before his arrest. What Ayushman had said about Sudarshan and Indu was bothering him. He was curious to know Ayush's version of what happened. He then goes and meets Indu to hear her version of things.

With the parts of the elephant now in place, he tries to reconstruct the events as seen by Ayushman, which led to the emergence of Rudransh.

❖❖❖

Residence, Karol Bagh

Around 4 months ago, 11 AM

Ayushman comes home at the end of the semester from college. Sudarshan asks him to clean the study room for him. Ayushman is cleaning the table, drawers, computer and books on the shelf. He picks up a book for cleaning, which is titled 'Love Story'. He likes the title, so he opens it and reads a remark in an elegant handwriting on the first page:

> *Just for you, an epic, straight from the heart. For treasured memories.*
>
> *Love,*
> *Indu*

Why has he kept this? Ayushman reads and feels unhappy about it.

❖❖❖

Residence, Karol Bagh

Around 2 months ago, 8 PM

Both Kritika and Ayushman are at home, this weekend. The family has planned a get together with friends for dinner. It is Shruti and Sudarshan's marriage anniversary. Sudarshan has invited his colleagues from office as well.

Before the cake cutting ceremony and dinner, they are having drinks and starters.

Indu and Sudarshan are talking in private in a corner.

"Thanks for all the help, Sudarshan."

He holds her hand. "Come on Indu. It was my duty. What are friends for?"

Ayushman comes to use the washroom. But he notices

Indu and Sudarshan together. *Why is Baba holding her hand?* Curious, he goes closer to them to hear the conversation:

"I feel so lonely."

"Don't ever feel alone. I will always be with you, no matter what."

Sudarshan notices Ayushman standing close by. He lets go of Indu's hand.

He is cheating on Mumma. Why does Mumma not do anything about it? A confused Ayushman walks away silently.

Residence, Karol Bagh
November 10, 6 PM

Sudarshan returns home after being released from CIU. There is no one at home. He leaves the door open and goes inside to take rest. He gets a call from Indu.

"Hi Indu."

"You were released from custody. Why didn't you tell anyone?"

"Who told you?"

"You had gone to meet Gopal today. He told me."

"So much has happened in the last few days, I just needed some time alone."

Ayushman enters the house. He sees the door open and thinks somebody is there. He hears a voice, so he walks slowly to see who it is. He realizes it is Sudarshan talking on the phone and starts to listen.

"Life has been very hard. I never thought they would let me go after I had confessed. But they let me go."

Sudarshan starts to cry.

"I know Indu. You are there for me."

He hangs up the phone. *He confessed about the affair and the murder of Mumma, but yet they let him go?* Angry and disgusted, he leaves.

Ten minutes later, Rudransh enters the home.

SI-3, CIU
November 30, 11:30 AM

Suryakant's father used to tell him about the dangers of half-truths. In his childhood, he was told that the course of the Kurukshetra war in the Mahābhārata was changed due to one half-truth. He recollects the story.

During the Kurukshetra war, after the defeat of Bhishma Pitamah, Dronacharya was appointed as the General of the Kaurava army. He was decimating the Pandava army. It was felt that if Dronacharya is not killed, there will be no Pandava army left. Everybody knew the love that Dronacharya had for his son Ashwathama. In order to kill him Lord Krishna hatched a plan.

The Kaurava army had a war elephant under the name of Ashwathama, Bheema was ordered to kill the elephant and announce the same to Dronacharya. On hearing this Dronacharya became distraught but he knew that Bheema could be lying. He turned to Yudhishthira who had a reputation of always speaking the truth and asked him whether what Bheema said was true.

Yudhishthira told Dronacharya that it was true that Bheema killed Ashwathama, but it was the elephant Ashwathama. But when Yudhishthira uttered 'but it was the elephant', Lord Krishna cleverly blew the war conch and Dronacharya could not hear it.

Due to the half-truth heard by him, Dronacharya became distraught with the death of his son and laid down his arms. In that moment, he was slayed by the Pandava general Drishtadyumna.

Truth without its context is *half-truth*. The greatest enemy of the truth is very often not falsehood, but half-truth. Much more dangerous. Much more lethal.

An idea is the most infectious virus known to humankind. Once a seed is sown, it is bound to manifest itself outwardly. *If only Ayushman had not heard the ardha-satya (half-truth)…*

Chapter 27
DVĀITA
(DUALISM)

Residence, Kirti Nagar
November 30, 7 PM

There is achievement and then there is contentment. Clearing UPSC and getting into IPS in his first attempt was an achievement, pleasing, but it wore off. What he was experiencing today was contentment - pleasing and lasting.

Suryakant was lying on his sofa. He had successfully solved his first case. More than success, it is the manner of the success which he is relishing. All because his heart ruled over his mind. His thoughts pan over his decision to come to India, his decision to join the IPS, his decision to join the CIU and the various decisions he took which helped him solve this mysterious case. *My heart has always been right.*

This case had given him more than he could ever

imagine. First and foremost - the respect of his team and his superiors. Then, he got to meet an illustrious and a bright mind in the form of Dr. Sudarshan Chatterjee. His regard and veneration for Sudarshan and his work had grown in leaps and bounds from his first encounter. Suryakant admired his wide knowledge on various subjects like psychology, chemistry and spirituality, as well as his ability to sync and synthesize this knowledge into practical life by creating Serum 801 and Serum 108. Kritika, who seems to be a perfect partner, had come into his life. *And the diary…* he thinks as he playfully strokes it, *I am the worthy successor to Neelkanth.* What he had learnt over the period of the last few weeks from Neelkanth had also been nothing less than extraordinary.

The case was done and it was now time to finish reading Neelkanth. He picks up the diary, flips it over and begins to read the third and the final part of the diary. This part for some reason has a lot of images, struck-off words, writings and re-writings. The first few pages are glued together and he has missed noticing these pages till now. He opens them and looks at the first page of the third part.

ll Vinaash ll

ll Satya ☯ Asatya ll

The symbol catches his attention.

He recognizes the symbol. It is the *"taichi* symbol" (literally "Diagram of the Supreme Ultimate"). *Taichi* symbol is a Chinese concept of duality describing how seemingly opposite or contrary forces may actually be complementary, interconnected, and interdependent in the natural world, and how they may give rise to each other as they interplay with one another. *Purusha* cannot exist without *Prakriti, Shiv* needs *Shakti.* Even the Deva-Asura dichotomy is a spiritual concept. The god (Deva) and anti-god (Asura), may sound as antagonistic forces at first, but they are narrative depictions of tendencies within ourselves. Just like satisfaction and greed, calmness and anger. Together they motivate a person. The equilibrium needs to be maintained.

The first part of the diary was conveying the duality, the connection he now sees.

Can Satya and Asatya be interdependent?

He flips to the next page and notices a strange picture. It is of a snake with some writings on it.

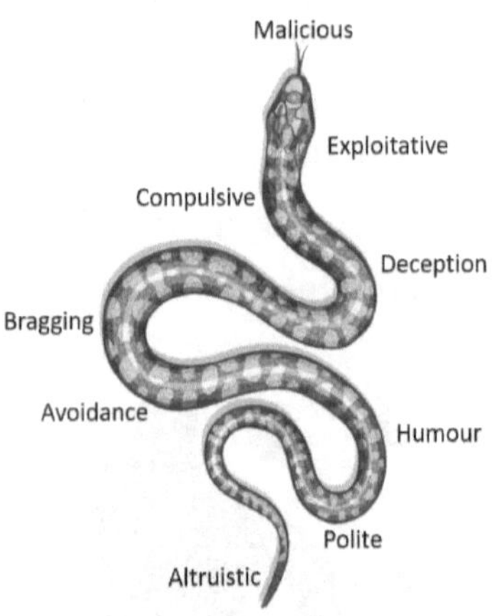

It appears to him that the image shows various types of lies in increasing degree of their severity.

Suryakant starts to read what Sudarshan had written on the earlier pages.

Pratyaksh: *Research has shown that the average number of lies told per day is 1.7. I believe that this number is too low and that many participants of this research were also lying about the extent of their lying.*

Humans tell lies for various reasons but not all of them are with a malicious intent.

Lying has an important role in society - it is one among the various "fictions" created by humans to live like a "social animal".

When human life shifted from individualistic to more cooperative ways, there was the birth of what is known as "social intelligence," and it changed the very way we behaved.

Suddenly, our psychological health started depending heavily on our social status within a particular group. We started to exaggerate and at times be Machiavellian. Both the behaviors involved a fair bit of lying. This was a natural part of human evolution. Not just humans, lying and deception are also well-known in the animal kingdom. Chameleons camouflage in response to their surroundings. Tigers and Cheetahs have markings to blend into the environment and be better predators. This helps us to hide weaknesses, escape danger and gain advantages in the struggle for resources. Nature has, thus, 'naturally' allowed this behavior to be 'selected' in the course of evolutionary process. Subjecting such acts of lying and deception to truth serum would thus hamper human evolution.

Anubhuti: *The notion of "lies = bad" and "truth =*

good" is an oversimplification of the usage of lies in our everyday life. Prosocial lies form an important part of our social mannerism. As an example, as part of day to day introductory greetings, we generally tend to have a "how are you?" step. This phase of the greeting is an important indicator of our relationship with others. If the other party is one's mother, the response to this would be elaborate, depending on whether or not one wants to share the burden of one's mental state with her. However, if the other party is an acquaintance, a polite "fine" will be a sufficient response. This is because as social beings, we have responsibilities to give certain categories of people, the relevant information, as per social norms. We lie when we have to withhold information in order to manage these complex relationships.

Similarly, well-placed serious lies can alleviate suffering. Lying is often about cost: it minimizes the cost and/ or maximizes the benefit to other people. For example, an employee may tell a colleague that they delivered an excellent presentation when they did not, or thank a gift giver for a gift they would have rather not received.

He turns over and then there was an altogether different reasoning by Sudarshan.

Anubhuti: What is truth? Is truth always "objective"? "Subjective" truth is what is true about one's experience of the world. How one feels when one sees the color red, what ice-cream tastes like to him, what it's like being with one's family, all these are one's own experiences and one's alone.

Sudarshan writes

Anubhuti: *Shruti has no idea what a banana tastes like to me, because I am not her and she cannot ever be in my head to feel what I feel. Though my love for Shruti has blossomed over time, imagine I being put to TS test every time I eat her "star" dish - banana pie, for which my fondness has only decreased over time. Sometimes the truth is messy and inconvenient. When Shruti asks me if she looks fat in her dress, I lie not only to protect her feelings, but also to avoid an avoidable conflict in my marriage and a lengthy discussion about diet and exercise.*

Suryakant stops and thinks for a while. *Sudarshan had particularly strong views about subjective truth and its impact on relationships. Are "lies" a necessity for human civilization, just like the "truth"? What is he trying to convey?*

Suryakant reads further.

Pratyaksh: *Lord Krishna in Karna Parva says even falsehood may be utterable where falsehood would become truth and truth would become falsehood. In a situation of peril to life and in saving one's marriage, falsehood becomes utterable. In a situation involving the loss of one's entire property, falsehood becomes utterable. When life is in danger, or for escaping from captivity by evil captors, or for the sake of a Dharma, falsehood may be uttered. These five kinds of falsehood have been declared to be sinless. On these occasions, falsehood would become truth and truth would become falsehood. He is a fool that practices truth without knowing the difference between truth and falsehood. Krishna told Kunti that Karna was the greatest archer warrior among* *her sons. But on Kurukshetra battlefield, he told Arjun that he was the greatest archer warrior to boost up the confidence of an already anxious Arjun.*

Suryakant takes a break and searches on his cell phone about what Krishna told Arjun in Karna Parva about lies. He comes across an interesting story in the Mahābhārata where Lord Krishna tells Arjun a story illustrating how speaking a harsh truth that causes harm to others is sinful. He starts to read it.

It is the story of Sage Kaushika who goes to hell for speaking the Truth. Lord Krishna describes a brahmana named Kaushika who took a vow to speak the truth at all times. He constructs a hut on the banks of Ganga and spends all his time praying and practicing meditation. He never speaks a single lie and becomes famous as a saint who always speaks the truth.

One day, a band of bandits come to his home, chasing a group of innocent people who were trying to escape the bandits and were seen by Kaushika. The bandits say to Kaushika, "Tell us in which direction have the people we are chasing gone?" Kaushika knew that if he spoke the truth, the bandits would find the innocent fleeing people and they would rob and kill them. But he thought that he must speak truthfully because he had taken a vow to speak the truth always. Therefore, upon being asked as to the whereabouts of these innocent people fleeing the bandits, Kaushika tells the bandits which direction the people went. As a result, the bandits capture the innocent victims and kill them.

Lord Krishna calls this "truthful" Kaushika a fool, who is ignorant of *Dharma.* His vow of speaking truth always caused harm to innocent people; and as a result of speaking this "truth", Kaushika went to hell.

The balance between Truth and Lie is "subtle". He returns to the diary.

Anubhuti: *As parents, we frequently tell kids not to lie. But that is not what we actually mean. For example, before we go over to a young Ayush's friend's house, I might tell him, "Remember, thank your friend for that compass box, and tell him how much you like it, even though you never use it." We claim that we try to teach our children not to lie, but in reality, we actually teach them how to lie, in a socially appropriate manner. This behavior is not merely tolerated; it is actually mandatory. Nobody will ever know if Shabri ke Ber (Shabri's berries) were actually sweet. Rama, in all his benevolence, nevertheless eats them and praises their taste to Shabri.*

If people stop trusting other people's actions to be what they appear to be, and instead incessantly question their motives and subject them to TS, social interactions would grind to a halt. It would destroy relationships and make the relationships mechanical. Would a doting husband be able to hide the reason for his absence at a movie date, because he was planning a surprise party for his wife's birthday, if he was subjected to TS?

Even business relationships would fail if every merger and acquisition, every advertising campaign, and every job interview involved administering TS. It would destroy the very fabric of society.

This serum would then become a Vish, a poison. Satyuga cannot be artificially brought in this Kaliyuga!

Sudarshan did not want his legacy to be one of the

"Destroyers of the society and its free will". *Interesting!*

He looks at the image of the snake with the degree of lies again. It is as if Sudarshan has appeared in his mind and is starting to tell him - *Truth Serum should only be used to destroy "Malicious lies" and not anything further.* The other lies must remain for the sake of free will of humans. They are essential to the fabric of our society and relationships. This is why TS is kept a secret, used only to defeat "malicious lies" for fighting crime and is not commercialized. If TS-108 is used to uncover other lies, it may lead to the collapse of the society itself.

The shishya now realizes what the guru has been trying to communicate all along. The true meaning of snake with the sword on the cover of the diary, is now revealed to him. He could feel Sudarshan telling him that the power could be a poison and it needs to be controlled. With this thought, he sees the image on the last page of the diary which he has noticed many times.

He notices a banyan tree with a *Guru* (teacher) and a *Shishya* (student). A banyan tree with its roots touching the ground, denotes the knowledge imparted by a *Guru* to his

Shishya sitting underneath it. The knowledge so imparted, stays even when the teacher might not be there and as a part of repaying his debt towards the teacher, the student is now spreading the knowledge ahead. The *Guru-Shishya* relationship is now complete.

It occurs to him that he has seen the tree before.

Chapter 28
Bhasmāsura
(One who killed himself)

Residence, Karol Bagh
November 30, 10 PM

Unlike a typical November night, there is relative warmth in the air tonight. The street is utterly silent as it is quite late. The white bungalow seems to be swathed in shadow, giving it a dark, gloomy look. No lights are on in the bungalow and it appears nobody is at home. Suryakant presses the bell. After a while, a light is turned on. Radhey comes and opens the door. Suryakant realizes that only Radhey is at home. *Kritika must be at her Noida residence for tonight.* He is pleased. Today, he wants to be alone.

Suryakant notices the 'Study' around the Banyan tree. He asks Radhey to open the Study and leave him alone. Radhey does as instructed. Moving slowly, he opens the door. He turns on the light and looks around. This room has been visited many times before by him. But tonight, is different.

Tonight, it is not a police officer that has come looking for evidence, but a *shishya* that has come looking for vidya. He looks around for a while. The place has already been searched. Then it occurs to him to move Sudarshan's table right under the tree. Pushing the table, he notices the flooring is constructed of tiles. One tile appears to be a bit odd. He uses his key chain to dig around the tile and finally elevates it. Inside it, there is a box. It is similar to the box that Sudarshan had left him in the locker. But this box has a 14-digit password. It is much more secure.

His hunch tells him that it must contain a far bigger secret. This time, he knows the password. It has to be 'NEELKANTH'.

He counts the number of digits in his mind. Carefully thinking, he slowly starts to punch the numbers '14 5 5 12 11 1 14 20 8'. As the open button is pressed, the box unlocks. The inside of the box is exactly the same as the earlier one.

It reveals another diary. On the first page of the diary there is a picture of Lord Shiva drinking the poison (that came out during the churning of *samudra manthan*) and becoming Neelkanth.

He takes a moment to absorb the thought again that the Truth Serum is poison.

The remaining pages contain everything he has ever wanted to know about TS-108. There is some movement which makes him look around to see if anybody is around. There is no-one. He places the box back, puts the tile at its original place and pushes the table back. Before leaving, he folds his hands and takes blessings from the Guru, one last time.

As he turns off the light, the study becomes dark.

But there is illumination inside.

Residence, Kirti Nagar
November 30, 11:30 PM

The key goes into the lock slowly and turns. The door opens. Suryakant quietly enters the room so as to not awaken Maa and sits on the sofa. He takes out the diary and starts reading it. It has the ingredients, the source, the chemical formulae, and the processes to prepare the TS-108 serum. He carefully reads the pages. An hour goes by in a flash.

He moves ahead turning the pages and notices that in the next few pages of the diary it is mentioned TS 1, TS 2, TS 3, TS 4, TS 5 and TS 6. *Is it related to the step-by-step development of TS-108?* But they are only six and have a date followed by some questions and answers. It then occurs to him. *TS must mean Test Subjects on whom he conducted the experiments.*

He starts to read the questions and answers.

TS 1: Feb 1, 2025

Did you cheat in the Mathematics paper in your final year in the 10th Board exams?
Yes

What is the password of your cell phone?
0108

Were you ever involved in a hit and run case?
Yes

Did your father beat you up in your childhood?
Yes

Have you developed a truth serum?
Yes

Do you like the banana pie made by Shruti?
No

Result - TS 1 has answered all the questions correctly. Test Successful.

Truth Serum and Banana pie. TS 1 is Sudarshan himself.

TS 2: March 1, 2025

Did you cheat in the Mathematics paper in your final year in 10th Board exams?
Yes

What is the password of your cell phone?
0108

Were you ever involved in a hit and run case?
No

Did your father beat you up in your childhood?
Yes

Have you developed a truth serum?
Yes

Do you like the banana pie made by Shruti?
No

Result - TS 2 has answered one question incorrectly. Second test within a month is not very accurate. The waiting period needs to be increased. The body and the mind tend to resist it, if used frequently.

Same set of questions. It is the second test he did on himself. This must be the reason, he instructed to use TS-108 only once.

<u>TS 3</u>: June 1, 2025

Did you cheat in the Mathematics paper in your final year in 10th Board exams?
Yes

What is the password of your cell phone?
0108

Were you ever involved in a hit and run case?
Yes

Did your father beat you up in your childhood?
Yes

Have you developed a truth serum?
Yes

Do you like the banana pie made by Shruti?
No

Result - TS 3 has answered correctly. Three months' gap looks sufficient.

It is the third test he did on himself. That's how he probably worked out the time gap needed between re-use of TS-108. Maybe he was being cautious and therefore asked it to be used only once.

TS 4: October 4, 2025

Did you ever steal from your father's wallet?
No

Have you ever smoked?
Yes

Do you take alcohol?
No

What is the password of your cell phone?
5879

The car dent on the bumper of my Maruti Dzire in June this year – was it you?
Yes

How did it happen?
While parking the car, instead of pressing the brake, I pressed the accelerator and the car hit the electricity pole.

Did you really read the book I had gifted you on your last birthday?
No

Do you have or had a boyfriend?
Don't have but had one in college

What was his name?
Shashwat Malik `

Result - TS 4 has answered all the questions correctly. Test Successful.

Suryakant recalls the conversation they had in the restaurant about their respective pasts. TS 4 must be Kritika.

<u>TS 5</u>: October 11, 2025

Did you ever steal from your father's wallet?
Yes

How much did you steal?
1000 rupees

Have you ever smoked?
Yes

Who taught you to smoke?
Kritika

Do you drink alcohol also?
No

What is the password of your cell phone?
2531

Do you have or had a girlfriend?
Yes, I have a girlfriend

What is her name?
Vaidehi Agarwal

Did you really read the book I had gifted you on your last birthday?
No

What is the name of your father?
———

Why no answer is written? It's left blank by him.

Result - TS 5 has answered all the questions correctly. Test Successful.

TS 5 must be Ayushman. What was Ayushman's answer to that question? Was this the reason that he changed his Will? Suryakant wonders.

TS 6: November 8, 2025

Where did we go for honeymoon after marriage?
We did not go for honeymoon

What are the names of your children?
Kritika and Ayushman

Which was the first dish you ever cooked for me?
Banana Pie

What is the password of your cell phone?
2407

Do you concur with my decision to mortgage our house for the sake of keeping my company afloat?
Yes

Result - TS 6 has answered all the questions correctly. Test Successful.

TS 6 must be Shruti.

He tested the serum on himself and his own family! *Why would he do that?* he contemplates. *May be because he wanted to keep its development and testing a secret. He probably wanted to know the answer to the last question and so tested it on Shruti. He broke his own rule!*

Suryakant keeps the diary down. He feels he has got the final missing piece of the puzzle. The date of the test on Ayushman is October 11th. He recalls the notes of psychiatrist which stated that on October 20th, Ayushman complained of his medications not working and a sudden increase in his violent tendencies. This date is just a few days after the first usage of TS-108 on him. Sudarshan's murder happened on November 10. The second murder of the PhD student happened few days after CIU injected him with TS-108. *This is the missing piece. TS-108 was the root cause behind the case. It led to side-effects in Ayush's mind, which resulted in his medications not working. And Shruti's accident happened on the same day after TS-108 was administered on her. Shruti had quit her teaching job due to health issues. Definitely, TS-108 had some side-effect with her medications or alcohol. It is too big of a coincidence to ignore!*

Suryakant is able to see everything clearly now. Sudarshan made something which helped destroy many criminals but the dangerous weapon destroyed not only him but also his whole family. Suryakant can't help comparing this to the story of Bhasmāsura. An *asura* (demon), Bhasmāsura, was granted by Lord Shiva the power to burn up and immediately turn into *bhasma* (ashes) anyone whose head he touched with his hand. The asura was tricked by God Vishnu's only female avatar, Mohini, the enchantress. Mohini tricked Bhasmāsura into touching his own head and he ended up turning himself into ashes.

His own power led to events that got him killed.

Is Lord Shiva trying to say something to me?

This knowledge is too big to be given to any individual. It can be an instrument of human liberation, but it can also be a weapon of destruction in the hands of any other individual, not as wise and worthy as Shiva. And God forbid the Government getting its hands on it or the public using it *en masse*, the society itself will crumble.

Suryakant realizes that the Truth Serum has to stay in the neck, it cannot be digested by the body. Else it will destroy everything. Probably, that's why Sudarshan named his research 'Neelkanth' - the one who could bear the poison - hold it in the neck and not swallow it, just like Lord Shiva held the poison in his neck protecting the body. Only someone as powerful and wise as Shiva - the Neelkanth

\- can bear this weapon and stay alive. *We humans, with our weaknesses, cannot.*

He looks at the photo of his father kept on the table for counsel. In that moment of meditative contemplation, it is as if his papa has spoken to him and he knows what needs to be done. His eyes move to the lighter kept right next to the photo.

Is this the difficult, life-altering choice that I was destined to make?

Let me trust my heart. My heart has always been right.

He picks up the lighter, lights it up and immerses the diary in the fire, turning the last memory of Sudarshan into ashes.

The clock ticks 1.08 AM.

EPILOGUE

Six months have elapsed.

Suryakant is sitting in his office staring at the wall clock. He is waiting for the day to end.

Suddenly, his phone buzzes. He is hoping it is Kritika. But it is a call from Vikram.

"Suryakant, are you coming to the party tonight at my home?"

"I will try, sir."

"What do you mean try! It's my wedding anniversary. You must come. Get Kritika along as well."

Suryakant answers softly, "Yes, sir."

"Great." Vikram disconnects the call.

How do I tell him that Kritika is not returning my messages? Suryakant wonders.

His thoughts are interrupted by a knock on the door. It is Brijesh.

"Sir, a new case is assigned to our Unit." Brijesh places the file on top of the stack of files already lying on his table. Realizing that Suryakant is lost in some thought, he leaves without saying anything further.

After a while, Suryakant gets up to leave. He is no longer enthused with the prospect of taking on a new case. His eyes nevertheless move to the file lying on the table.

It reads 'Case No. 108'. The number captures his

attention. His hand moves to pick up the file but he stops midway.

Making a decision is easy. To live with it, is the real test. With the diary, the legacy of Sudarshan has also turned to ashes. CIU is functional but has nearly exhausted its special power.

The last six months have seen the number of unsolved cases rise to forty percent, highest since CIU's formation. A mother grieves for a dead daughter, a father searches for a missing teenage son, a husband claims innocence regarding his dead wife and a bank hunts for its robbers. But none seems to be getting the answers they are looking for. There is no justice for their loss. The media is crying incompetent police yet again. The pressure is mounting on the police to give answers.

He may have burnt it, but Suryakant, the chosen heir, continues to live with the secrets of the diary buried deep within him. What's inside the mind can never be burnt. An enormous power, once tasted, is difficult to let go. His photographic memory is his power, his curse.

What is born, shall die. What is dead, shall never die.

Will the Neelkanth rise again?

ABOUT THE AUTHORS

Satyam Srivastava (born 13th October, 1982) is an Indian author. He is an Indian Revenue Service (IRS) officer of 2011 batch. He completed his B. Tech and M. Tech from IIT Mumbai in Electrical Engineering in 2005. He worked in the private sector at Bangalore for 6 years before he qualified in the Civil Services Examination. He has worked in various capacities in Govt. of India in diverse areas such as investigation, assessment and tax administration. Playing lawn tennis and reading fiction are his key interest areas.

Rajeev Garg (born 29th June, 1986) is an Indian author. He is an Indian Revenue Service (IRS) officer of 2011 batch. He completed his B. Tech from Pondicherry Engineering College in Electronics & Communication Engineering in 2008. He has worked in various capacities in Govt. of India in diverse areas such as Corporate Taxation, International Taxation and Transfer pricing. He is an avid reader with interests in quizzing and photography.

Both the authors are engineers turned career bureaucrats. They are batchmates and good friends.